I0772601

# TIMELESS PARADOX

# Novels By Bernard Cenney:

Sparrow's Tears

Close Your Eyes And See

Timeless Terror

Timeless Soldier

Timeless Embrace

Timeless Destiny

Timeless Paradox

# *TIMELESS PARADOX*
# BERNARD CENNEY

## AUTHOR'S NOTE:

This literary manuscript is entirely a work of fiction.  Any similarity or resemblance to businesses, organizations, places, names, characters, real persons, incidents, or events is purely coincidental, unintentional, imaginary, or used in a fictitious manner.

In Memoriam:

JAMES B. CENNEY
19 OCT 1989 — 11 OCT 2004

Loved Forever

Send your tax deductible contributions to find a cure for children's hypertrophic cardiomyopathy to:

www.childrenscardiomyopathy.org

Thank you.
Bernard Cenney

Dedication:

Special thanks go to my wife, Kongsri Cenney.

Over thirty-eight years ago in Southeast Asia, Kongsri left her family, her country, and everything that was familiar to her in order to marry a young American Special Forces Captain.  She took my hand and never looked back.  We have supported each other in conflict and peace, hardship and success, sorrow and joy.  Through it all she has loved me unconditionally and never left my side.

Bernard Cenney
Lt. Colonel (Retired)
United States Army

PREFACE:  15

PART ONE:  25

PROLOGUE:  BERLIN 1945:  29

     1.  TIME ENDS NOW:  45

     2.  VISIONS:  55

     3.  WHITE HOUSE BRIEFING:  69

     4.  MSS:  85

     5.  WARLOCK:  97

     6.  A FRIEND:  107

PART TWO:  121

     7.  WHERE AM I?:  125

     8.  MOSSAD:  135

     9.  BRAINWASHING:  143

    10.  THE PLAN:  155

    11.  HEALING MINDS CENTER:  165

    12.  MANCHURIAN CANDIDATE:  177

    13.  DIPLOMATIC SECURITY:  189

    14.  TRIGGER:  199

PART THREE:  211

    15.  STRANGER:  215

    16.  PARADOX:  223

    17.  MASTER PLAN:  237

    18.  GOOD GUYS WEAR BLACK:  253

    19.  A DEBT PAID:  265

    20.  TIMELESS PARADOX:  279

EPILOGUE:  TIME STARTS NOW:  301

# PREFACE

was. After he died, I thought the world would end. In my mind, I waited for the end to come. But it didn't. People went to work, children went to school, and life kept grinding on. My mind tore to pieces over whether to stop moving or to keep pushing onward.

My wife and daughters were suffering terribly as well, perhaps even more than me. Together as a family, we comforted and supported each other. I don't believe it would have been possible for me to move on without the love of my family. I felt that I had to show strength for them. I had to be the father to push everyone onward and hold the family together. If I gave up, I would have failed everyone. I knew that I had to control my grief and move forever onward. These were the thoughts constantly pounding through my mind.

James' death started me to think deeply, perhaps for the first time in my life, and to read incessantly. I read *The Upanishads*, *The Tibetan Book of the Dead*, and *The Bible*. I studied the Greek historians and philosophers: Aeschylus, Aristotle, Epictetus, Herodotus, Plato, and Sophocles. I read works by Billy Graham, Dalai Lama, Deepak Chopra, Dr. Melvin Morse, and Dr. Raymond Moody, to name just a few. I devoured just about any book that dealt with the subject of reincarnation and life after death. *The New Testament* was the enlightened example to me that life is suffering, and you must force yourself through the pain and move forward.

Pain and suffering must be understood and fully absorbed. You cannot deaden the feelings. You cannot even attempt to understand life without suffering. The message I gleaned from *The Gospel of John* brought hope to me. Sometimes a spiritual transcendence can occur from experiencing intense sorrow.

What I understood for myself was disconcerting. Tragedy strikes everyone. Those who think they are immune, only have but to wait. It will come. More tragedy is lingering around the corner. Life is the great equalizer. You cannot barter for a better life. You must push on through tragedy with all the strength you have inside. Despite unanswered prayers, you must forever move forward and do what's right. To be alive is to have constant pain and struggle.

You must push yourself forward. You must pray. You must master discipline. You must keep focus. You must practice compassion. You must hone understanding. You must think. Learn to speak less, and listen more. Put others first and yourself second. Try to help as many people as you can in your life, and if you can't help them at least don't hurt them. The best possible life you can have is one of helping others, and constantly striving to do what is right, regardless of the outcome.

How do you know what is right? Search your heart. Buddha is about compassion; Jesus is about love. Put those together and it's pretty powerful. Treat everyone with dignity, respect, love, and compassion. The reward you receive is the knowledge and peace of mind that you did what was right.

I spent a career in the US Army continually taking and giving orders, and telling soldiers what to do. I came to an understanding that I could not control events. All I could do was try to lead a good life, help others, and set a positive example. I have failed over and over again. My joy comes from helping others when I can, and watching my children excel and lead good lives.

Now to the subject of my novels.

Writing the books *Sparrow's Tears, Close Your Eyes and See, Timeless Terror, Timeless Soldier, Timeless Embrace, Timeless Destiny,* and *Timeless Paradox* became therapy for me — the best therapy. When I think of my son James, I see him always helping others — those who could not help themselves — whether at home or in school. He made me realize that nothing is without purpose; that there is a majestic plan which unfolds itself across the vastness of time equally embracing each life, no more or less important than another. Writing the novels became my way of honoring and paying tribute to James. It allowed me to envision him as an adult, giving him the type of life I would have wished for him. Writing the books allowed me to dream my son a life which I felt had ended too quickly. James Cenney is alive in the pages of my novels. He encourages my readers and me to move forever forward in life.

The hero of my novels — Captain James Ross — is patterned after my son. They both have the same looks, style, loves, and ambience. They are both heroes. But even more than that, as my son James Cenney would say, they "… are intelligent human beings."

My fervent hope is that veterans who are suffering from PTSD and depression can use fiction writing as therapy.

Bernard Cenney
Floresville, Texas

# TIMELESS PARADOX

# PART ONE

*Do not act as if you had ten thousand years to throw away.  Death walks with you, arm-in-arm.  Be good while you live and when you can.*

Marcus Aurelius Antoninus
121 — 180 AD
Roman Emperor

# PROLOGUE

# BERLIN 1945

Berlin was under siege from the Russian Red Army. The First Belorussian Front commanded by Marshall Zhukov was advancing from the east and north. Marshall Konev's First Ukrainian Front was advancing towards Berlin in the south. The idea was to simply obliterate the capital city of Hitler's thousand-year Third Reich. The Berlin garrison was short on soldiers, and was being augmented with Hitler Youth and Volkssturm members. The Volkssturm was a national militia implemented since Germany was short of young conscriptable men. It consisted of pre-teens and the elderly. Their mission was to salvage victory with a violent burst of fanatic rage. But, in reality all they really could hope for was to buy time and hold back the Russians for as long as they could.

Hans Kammler glanced at the Wehrmacht issued Phenix watch on his left wrist. He could barely make out the dial since the watch had long ago lost its water resistance, and the crystal was now fogging up.

*Damn it!* he thought. *I've got to get through!*

Obergruppenführer Hans Friedrich Kammler served the Third Reich with distinction. As a member of the Schutzstaffel or SS, Kammler managed engineer requirements, and was in charge of the Special Projects Division for the Führer. Special Projects included the Führer's wonder-weapons. These wunderwaffe were Hitler's gift to the future. Kammler oversaw everything, from the revolutionary Horten 229 jet flying wing aircraft to the breathtaking V-2 missile attack systems. Hans Kammler was one of the esteemed Councilors of the Interior.

Tonight he was speeding through the rain drenched streets of Berlin in his Mercedes-Benz SSK roadster, splashing buckets of mucky water everywhere.

*Maybe this rain will slowdown the Russian advance. The damned barbarians were slaughtering everyone and everything in their path. Russian soldiers were raping every German woman they could find between eight and eighty. This wasn't war. It was a nightmare, it was Dante's Inferno, it was Goethe's Faust!*

Kammler furrowed his brow and thought to himself.

*It's good to know that the Führer is still in charge. I know he's got a plan for final victory — and I am part of that plan.*

He quickly downshifted and swerved to avoid a dead horse in the middle of the road.

Kammler brought his Mercedes-Benz sloshing to a halt in front of the huge Reich's Ministry of Science and Technology building. He slipped out of the roadster and tossed the keys to the black uniformed SS-Unterscharführer standing guard.

"Here, take care of it."

The SS guard adeptly caught the keys and immediately gave the Nazi salute.

"Sieg heil," said the guard.

Kammler instantly stopped and returned the salute.

"Heil Hitler," he hurriedly replied.

Sprinting up the concrete steps, Kammler mused to himself.

*Operation Chronos is complete.*

*My physicists have finished putting Die Glocke prototypes through their final test runs.*

*Full-scale production has begun.  I already have three machines primed.*

Everything happens in time.

The Greek word for 'time' is *chronos*.

Chronos was considered a God in pre-Socratic Greek philosophy, and was the son of Uranus — God of the sky.  Chronos wounded his father, and from the blood was born the Furies — female spirits of vengeance and justice.

The Nazis were obsessed with Teutonic and Norse myths.

In Norse mythology, the world was depicted as a tree — the tree of the world — known as Yggdrasil.  Odin's Kingdom of the Nine Realms was attached to Yggdrasil.  Chronos has been depicted as a serpent wrapped around Yggdrasil.  The world will come to an end when the serpent lets go of Yggdrasil, or so it was believed in ancient times.

Operation Chronos was the codename for Nazi Germany's secret attempt to master space-time vortex compression.

The Third Reich was using German Professor Albert Einstein's special and general relativity laws of physics for gravity as a curvature of space-time, and the relationship of time to gravity absence.

The experiments utilized thorium-nitrate emulsion, beryllium-peroxide fusion, xerum-methane separation, and mercury displacement. His scientists had produced the desired magnetic field separation outcomes at high intensity counter-rotating speeds. Nazi physicists and mechanical engineers had solved the issue of antigravity time dilation. The Henge test site was used for the antigravity propulsion trials. Success had been achieved.

The resulting manufactured device was about the size and weight of a sedan, only more so resembling a very large bell. Hence, its German codename became *Die Glocke,* or in English simply 'the Bell.' All this had been accomplished at the Riese facility near the Czechoslovakian border.

Now General Kammler was at the top of the stairs as two young SS-Sturmmann guards flung open the seventeen-foot-tall richly polished mahogany double doors, exposing the colossal marble foyer of the Third Reich's Ministry of Science and Technology.

Kammler was an engineer. He was a realist. He believed in what he could build and see.

But Chronos was different.

Chronos could be proved theoretically on the chalk board, but had the capacity to enter the realm of something mystical — something magical. It was as if science and magic had blended together.

As he hurried along, Kammler pondered to himself.

*Time won't matter anymore.*

*We will own time. We will bring the past and present together. Operation Chronos will change the history of the world.*

Kammler approached his laboratory and was once again saluted by the SS soldiers standing guard at the door.

*Tonight I will test Die Glocke,* he thought, as he fumbled with his keys in the lock.

*Tonight I will take the first trip through time.*

Kammler opened the twin doors and quickly walked inside the huge expanse of laboratory. There resting on pallets was the machine known as Die Glocke. He stopped in front of it and was in awe of his work.

The device was approximately nine feet wide and fifteen feet tall. It was constructed from a combination of beryllium, magnesium, titanium, and aluminum alloys. It looked heavy, and weighed approximately four thousand pounds. Its color was a faded dark metallic gray. Electronic cables crisscrossed around its base and up to its top. There was a hatch with a nautical locking wheel on the front of it. Circling around the convex top of the machine were reflecting heat shields.

Kammler spun open the hatch and stepped inside. He reclined back in the contoured Luftwaffe pilot seat and buckled himself in with the fallschirmjäger harness. He looked at his Phenix watch and noted the time.

*Midnight.*

Anticipating the unexpected, Kammler powered up the machine. He observed the Macht Auf gauge start to glow an ancient yellow luminescence.

*Yellow always means yield.*

*I've come too far for any concern now.*

Kammler had both hands on the cold metal of the Gangschaltung control lever.

*Backwards or forwards?* thought Kammler to himself.

*Into the past or into the future?*

*Forward,* he thought.

Then he pressed the Trolit Thermoplast button on top, and ratcheted the shifter lever forward.

*Clack, clack, clack.*

The sounds coincided with the spinning of the control panel mechanical sprocket calendar.

*Clack, clack, clack.*

If Kammler could have seen the outside of Die Glocke, he would have been amazed.

The base of the machine was emitting a greenish-orange glow, and the entire outer capsule was starting to vibrate.

The clacking sound inside was in competition to a swirling, rushing, windstorm sound growing in intensity outside.

Inside Die Glocke, Kammler's body was immediately flushed with an overwhelming sense of peaceful bliss.

The SS guards outside the door heard the noises and looked at each other.

"What is happening?" one guard asked.

"Herr General is testing the machine again," the other replied.

The two men looked at each other and nodded.

But the noises grew louder, much louder.

"We better take a look," the bolder of the two said.  "Maybe Herr General needs help."

The other guard thought for a second.

"Very well, why not?"

They opened the door and the two SS guards walked inside the laboratory.

Looking around, they saw that Kammler's scientific papers were strewn about everywhere helter-skelter.

The SS guards walked carefully forward and stood in front of the spot where Die Glocke had just been seconds earlier.

There they stared down at the concrete floor and saw a sizzling, steaming, crystallized sheet of glass.  But General Hans Kammler and the machine codenamed Die Glocke were nowhere to be found.

The bolder of the two Nazi guards crouched down looking at the crystallized floor and said, "Mein Gott."

# PRESENT DAY

*We are always in a hurry to be happy, for when we have suffered a long time, we have great difficulty in believing in good fortune.*

Alexandre Dumas
1802 — 1870
French Novelist
The Count of Monte Cristo

# CHAPTER ONE

# TIME ENDS NOW

Lin walked out of the ladies room and into the dark noisy lounge.

Watching the couples joining and becoming one on the dance floor, she peered through the smoky air, searching for Ross.

I *can feel James here,* she thought.

Then she sees him, sitting at a far corner table, alone, waiting.

Trying hard to control her heart, she walks over to him.

There they meet, softly, gently, reassuringly.

"Hello Mister," says Lin.

Teasingly she asks, "Are you waiting for anyone?"

Ross stands up.

"Yes I am.  I'm waiting for my love," he says.

"Here," says Lin taking his hand, "let me show you where it is."

They move to the dance floor and embrace.

Two hearts become one as they start swaying to the music.

Slowly at first, ever slowly.

They look deeply into each others eyes.

"What are you thinking about Lin?" asks Ross.

"Us," she replies.

"What are you thinking about Jamie?"

"You," replied Ross.

Then he leans in and they kiss.

Soon time stands still.

They dance until the music stops and then return to their table. Ross holds out a chair for Lin and then takes his seat. He reaches for his champagne glass and gulps it down.

"It's been quite a day hasn't it Lin?" said Ross as he wraps his arm around her.

Lin leans her head against his shoulder. "It sure has," said Lin. "I'm glad the Longinus Spear is safe and back inside the Hofburg Palace where it belongs."

Ross nodded his head.

A quizzical expression appeared on his face.

Lin sensed something was wrong.

Looking in his eyes, Lin asked, "What's the matter James?"

Ross shook his head.

"Not sure," he said. "All of a sudden my head feels kinda fuzzy."

Ross pressed his left thumb and forefinger to the bridge of his nose and squeezed, tightly closing his eyes. He shook his head and tried to clear his mind.

"I feel dizzy, like I'm gonna pass out," said Ross.

Lin Sparrow knew the dangerous game of fighting international terrorism that her fiancé was involved in, and she accepted it. She was also a nurse and her medical instincts immediately took over. She reached forward and picked up Ross's champagne glass.

Lin ran her index finger around the inside rim of the glass and touched it to her tongue. Her eyes grew wide.

"Flunitrazepam," she said.

Flunitrazepam, also known as the date-rape drug, is a powerful benzodiazepine hypnotic with a potency ten times that of diazepam.

Lin stared back at Ross who looked like he would pass out.

"Come on, we've got to get out of here," she said.

Lin pushed her chair back and got up. She put Ross's arm around her shoulders and stood him up.

Ross was willfully fighting the effects of the sedative.

*Focus,* Ross thought to himself, *focus damn it.*

"Come on James, one step at a time," said Lin. "One foot in front of the other. We've got to get you back to the room."

*One foot in front of the other,* thought Ross. *Keep moving. Move forward. Keep going soldier.*

Lin struggled with Ross, half pulling and half dragging him to the exit.

"Come on Jamie," said Lin.

The maître d' saw what was happening and hurried over.

"May I be of assistance, mademoiselle?" asked the maître d'.

"Um yes, can you help me with my boyfriend? I'm afraid he's had a little too much to drink," said Lin.

"Bien sûr, mademoiselle," answered the maître d'. He placed his arm around Ross, and together they moved him to the lobby and sat him down on a plush sofa.

Ross felt like he was starting to lose consciousness.

*Focus,* he told himself. *Keep focusing.*

Ross dug his fingers deeply into the plush sofa cushions. He tilted his head back and started to gulp in breaths of air.

Lin checked Ross's pulse.

*Erratic and fading,* she thought.

Then Lin struck Ross openhanded across his face.

*SLAP!*

Lin's hand left a red mark on Ross's cheek, but the slap did nothing.

Ross wobbled from side to side and couldn't catch his breath.

Lin knelt down and checked Ross's pulse again while lifting one of his eyelids.

"Call an ambulance!" Lin shouted to anyone who would listen.

The very worried looking maître d' immediately pulled out his cellphone and started punching in the number.

"I'm calling right now, I'm calling," he said hurriedly.

Ross started gasping while trying to suck in air.

"Ahh," whispered Ross, "can't … catch … my … breath …"

He felt the pressure in his chest grow like it would burst his heart.

The maître d' said, "The ambulance will be here in four minutes mademoiselle."

Confusion overtook Ross as his body lapsed into physiological shock.

Ross started to slip off of the sofa. Lin grabbed him and eased him to the floor. His eyelids fluttered once more and he feebly tried to reach out to Lin but couldn't.

With his fiancée Lin Sparrow's beautiful face as his last thought, Captain James Ross slipped into unconsciousness and passed out on the floor like a rag doll.

# CHAPTER TWO

# VISIONS

58

The ambulance brought Ross to the Vienna General Hospital, located at Währinger Gürtel 18-20, 1090 Wien, just three miles away. Lin had sat in front next to the driver during the trip, and immediately jumped out once they arrived at the emergency room. A gurney was already waiting outside. Next to the gurney stood four medical personnel, all wearing long white lab coats and baby blue scrubs.

*Curious,* thought Lin. *They're all Asian.*

The ambulance paramedics quickly opened the rear door and transferred Ross, with intravenous fluids and oxygen attached, to the waiting gurney. Lin took a hold of Ross's hand and held it during the transfer.

"We'll take it from here mademoiselle," said one of the Vienna General attendants with a heavy Asian accent.

Lin glanced at his nametag.

*Dr Wu Qiang.*

Lin blurted out, "He passed out and had trouble breathing.  I think he was drugged."

Wu Qiang conversed to his three assistants in Mandarin.  They quickly wheeled Ross's gurney inside the emergency room and straight to a bank of elevators.  Lin followed closely.

"I think the drug was flunitrazepam," she said.

Doctor Wu Qiang extracted a pen and wrote something down on his clipboard.

"And who are you, mademoiselle?"

"I'm Lin, Lin Sparrow," she said.  "Don't you want to know who your patient is?"

The doctor smiled revealing bad teeth, and then read from his clipboard.

"Mister James Ross," said Wu.  "We got his name from the Herrenhof Steigenberger Hotel when they notified us of the emergency.  Is that correct?"

"Yes," said Lin.

The elevator doors hissed open and Wu turned to Lin and said, "I'm sorry, but this is as far as you go."  He pointed with his clipboard. "Our waiting room lounge is around the corner and to the left.  You can make yourself comfortable there."

Lin pleaded, "But I want to go with James."

The attendants already had Ross inside the elevators.

"I'm afraid that's impossible.  We're taking him to ER number three.  What is your phone number?"

Lin gave her number to the doctor and he wrote it down.

"We will call you as soon as he is out of danger."

Then Doctor Wu Qiang smiled and reassured her.

"Don't worry.  He will be fine.  We'll take good care of him," said Wu.  Then he entered the elevator and nodded to the others.  The doors hissed shut.

Lin stood looking at the closed elevator doors and exhaled deeply.  Then she turned and walked down the hall to the waiting room.

The waiting room was empty.  Lin looked at the clock on the wall and saw that it was almost two o'clock in the morning.  She felt in her pocket for the Beretta pistol she had slipped out of James' suit coat before the ambulance arrived.

*Good thing I got this,* she thought.  *It would be hard to explain to the hospital staff.*

At first she sat down on a vinyl couch, but then the stress of the day overwhelmed her and she put up her feet and sprawled out.  She was soon fast asleep.

Lin Sparrow tossed and turned on the couch.  Sweat was beading on her forehead.  A low guttural moan emanated from her throat and pushed through her pursed lips.  Lin began dreaming.


Lin was with James Ross, her fiancé.  They were on a beach strolling together, hand in hand.  It was a lazy day, sun drenched, and filled with hopes and dreams of the future.

Time to fall in love.

Time to live their life.

Together — forever.

Lin looked into his eyes and smiled.  Ross smiled back, and everything seemed right with the world.

But now the beach suddenly turned into a fog.  A misty gray, all-encompassing fog.

Lin and Ross stepped into the fog and she soon lost her grip on his hand.  Ross just vanished.

But now the fog began to clear, as if someone had waved a magic wand.  Lin looked and saw two figures emerging.  The figures had auras around them.  Lin stared at the figures harder.  They were both James Ross.

*Two!*

*Something is wrong!*

*This can't be!*

One James had a yellow aura, and the other had black.

Yellow means someone is a natural leader, are motivational and positive, exude confidence and joy, and are on the path to spiritual awakening.  Black meant someone who is holding onto trauma, disturbed, or has dark forces guiding them.

And then she saw it and gasped.

A funeral procession.

A State funeral procession.

The day grew overcast and the fog came back.

Flags were gently flapping in the breeze.

*Clip-clop, clip-clop.*

Lin could feel the sound the horses hooves made on the asphalt.

The military caisson carried the deceased to his final resting place over the bridge and up the hill to Arlington National Cemetery.

Lin now began to shiver on the hospital couch as the dream continued.

Suddenly the sky lit up with a huge blue-green video screen. Splashing across it in blood-red lettering were messages.

"Israel is defeated."

"Taiwan falls to Chinese aggression."

"Hero Green Beret turns traitor."

"Assassin identified as James Ross."

*What in the world is this?*

*What has happened?*

*This is a nightmare!*

*This can't be!*

*Something's wrong!*

*Something is terribly, horribly wrong!*

*Nooooooooooooo!*

Lin Sparrow awoke at five o'clock in the morning with the jolt of an electric spark. Her forehead was glistening with trickles of cold salty sweat. She sat up on the hospital waiting room couch and shook her head.

*I remember a restroom close by,* she thought.

Lin stood up and walked out of the waiting room and into the hall.

*There it is.*

Once inside, Lin clicked on the lights and examined her face in the mirror above the porcelain sink.

*This is crazy.*

*Something's not right.*

*I can see it.*

*I can feel it.*

*I can sense it.*

*I know it.*

*My mother said I was a seer.*

*My father said I had the gift.*

*I've always had it.*

*Back home, our neighbors called it witchcraft.*

*Others called it clairvoyance.*

*Whatever its name — I've got it.*

She knew her dreams were more than nightmares or visions.

They were memories.

She reached into her purse and pulled out a tiny tube of minty Crest toothpaste and squeezed a dab onto her pink toothbrush. Lin brushed her teeth quickly.

Lin stared deeply into the brown eyes analyzing her in the mirror.

She was five-feet-nine-inches tall.

That was tall for a Malaysian lady.

But Lin was only half Malay.

She was a mixture of East and West, just like her American boyfriend Captain James Ross.

Lin's mother, Mira Wan Tengku, was Malay, and her father, Lieutenant Alastair Jasper Sparrow, had been a British Special Air Service officer assigned to their embassy in Kuala Lumpur. He was killed from a terrorist bomb explosion when Lin was just a child. She had never really gotten to know her father all that well. Her mother never remarried, and had kept the last name of Sparrow.

Lin was twenty-six years old now.

She continued staring at herself in the mirror.

Her silky raven locks cascaded slightly below her shoulders, with bangs that stopped just above her eyebrows. She had long sexy eyelashes, and a petite nose that was slightly upturned. Her eyes were deep brown almonds that sparkled in the light, and her mouth was large and captivatingly beautiful, with glistening full lips. Her skin was very smooth with almost no body hair. As with most Asian women, her legs were naturally satiny smooth and never required shaving. She kept her fingernails cut short and unpainted, however she did apply a clear polish to her toenails. Her calves were muscled, her stomach flat, and at times she exhibited unusual strength.

Lin used to serve as Executive Personal Secretary to the Honorable Simon Watlington, the United States Ambassador to Malaysia. That was also when she first met James Ross. That civil service job had been rewarding, but at a cost to her dignity and self-respect. It just became too unbearable for her to work at the US Embassy in Kuala Lumpur. She simply could not stand to work, day after day, within the labyrinth of backstabbing political machinations. Lin had always wanted a job that she could be proud of. She wanted to do something that would make a difference in people's lives. She wanted to have a sense of actually helping people, of making the world a little better place to live in. She wanted to give something of herself back to the people of Malaysia. Consequently, she enrolled in an accelerated evening studies program at the Puteri Nursing College, and completed her Bachelor of Science in Nursing degree. She served for a time as a critical care registered nurse in the emergency room of the Twin Towers Medical Center for Doctor Arjinderpal Sekhon in Kuala Lumpur, Malaysia. But then she started to have more dreams and visions — dreams and visions which included her then-boyfriend, James Ross, and which led to more and more adventures. Adventures which carried her across the globe and literally into and out of the jaws of death. And then Ross had proposed marriage, and she had accepted.

*Am I really engaged to this man?*

*Is this for real?*

*Am I really here?*

She had to be sure, since just last night she and Ross and Lon Inus had killed four members of a Chinese spy team who were attempting to steal the Spear of Destiny and the Nazi time machine.

Lin was now engaged to James Ross.

*Captain and Mrs. James Ross,* she mused.

*He was on leave from the US Army.*

*We should be planning our wedding.*

*We should be looking forward to a life together.*

*Together.*

*Forever.*

But instead, Lin was in a waiting room at Vienna General Hospital waiting to hear how Ross was doing.

*I know it was Flunitrazepam. He had to have been drugged in the lounge.*

Lin thought for a second …

She knew Ross was twenty-nine years old.

*He's really tall too, probably six-foot-three I would guess, and around a hundred and eighty-five pounds or so.*

*With lovely piercing dark brown eyes, and sexy shards of brown hair hanging across his forehead that would never stay in place.*

*He was half Thai, half caucasian.*

*He was a Captain in the United States Army Special Forces.*

*He saved my life.*

*And I love him.*

*Oh I love him so.*

Lin nervously fingered the engagement ring Ross had given her. It was a one carat diamond, set in a four prong, eighteen karat gold ring.

Lin Sparrow's dreams had always turned out to be metaphors for the truth. They were in fact visions of a possible future. A future, that if not changed, if not acted upon, would materialize as the present.

Lin started pacing about. She looked at her Citizen Eco-Drive ProMaster Dive watch.

*Five-thirty.*

*It has been over three and a half hours since James was brought in.*

Lin knew someone should have come and advised her as to Ross's status by now.

*This is not right.*

# CHAPTER THREE

# WHITE HOUSE BRIEFING

Snow fell the night before, and a crunchy glistening blanket of it transformed Lafayette Park and the South Lawn into a frosty winter wonderland.  Washington DC was gorgeous this time of year for those who worked around the clock to secure freedom.  For many, the seat of power for that freedom is in the Executive Branch of the United States, otherwise known as the Office of the President.  Since the year 1800 with the Presidency of John Adams, the official residence of every American President has been the White House.

Located at 1600 Pennsylvania Avenue NW in Washington DC — the White House complex includes the Executive Residence, the East Wing, the West Wing, the Eisenhower Executive Office Building, and a guest residence known as Blair House.  The President's Executive Residence has six stories, two of which are underground.  The first floor of the West Wing includes the Oval Office, from which the President conducts his most sensitive work.

The interior decor and seating arrangements can vary, but in the Oval Office today there were two large three-seat beige sofas facing each other and parallel to the President's famous Resolute Desk. This morning the Oval Office was hosting a flurry of classified activity.

Classified?

Executive Order 13526 established the US classification information system. Top Secret is the highest level of classified information there is. To publicly reveal such information is said to cause grave harm to the national security. Even certain Top Secret information is further broken down into Sensitive Compartmented Information, or SCI. This type of information can be openly read inside a Sensitive Compartmented Information Facility, or SCIF. The Oval Office meets this strict criteria. It is not uncommon for classified information to be kept close-hold for various reasons — many of them political. Information is power, or so it is said.

Spread out on the couches facing each other were four of President Donald Trump's most trusted colleagues. They were: Chief of Staff of the Army General Braxton Matthews, Director of the National Security Agency (NSA) Teresa Cenni, Director of the Central Intelligence Agency (CIA) Anna Kliner, and Counselor to the President, Metta Ngernluan.

Metta Ngernluan's family legally immigrated to the United States from Laos when she was only two years old. Her father taught physics at Central Michigan University, and her mother was an accomplished concert pianist. Metta became a piano virtuoso by the age of five, and graduated magna cum laude from Harvard Law School at the age of twenty-three. She resigned as Team Chief of the Law Division of the

Ford Motor Company when President Trump came calling. Metta was happy with her choice. She found President Trump to be a most engaging, sincere, and honest leader.

"Thank you all for coming today. Let's just start with Metta, okay?" said President Trump.

The Counselor to the President cleared her throat.

"Sir," said Metta, "President Xi Jinping will meet with you tomorrow evening in Vienna. On the plate is expansion of the Abraham Accords, increasing tariffs and economic sanctions, Hamas containment and increased arms sales to Israel, and halting China's US land-grab."

President Trump was leaning forward in his chair and was, as usual, listening intently and with complete focus.

"Right. I'm ready for him. Thanks. Go on," he said.

"Sir, Russia has withdrawn the remainder of its forces from Ukraine since your last discussion with President Putin," said Metta.

"I knew he would," said Trump. "He saw the light."

"Yes sir. The remainder of the border wall has been installed, and coupled with our zero-tolerance policies the Border Patrol is now reporting less than fifty illegal crossings per month," said Metta proudly.

"Great," replied the President. "I knew it."

Metta smiled.

"Crime is down 25% in Republican governed states since you last addressed the nation."

President Trump asked, "What about New York and California?"

Metta looked at her spreadsheet.

"Unfortunately Governors Newsom and Hochul's policies remain the same. Smash and grab crime is pretty much rampant, and violent crime is up."

"Yeah," said President Trump, "such a shame. They need new governors that's all."

Metta smiled and said, "The strategic oil reserves have been refilled and the Democrats are screaming bloody murder."

Trump chuckled.

"The price of oil is down, and gasoline is at a national average of $1.87 per gallon. Your tax cuts are working and spending is up. Inflation has reached an all time low of 1.3%."

Metta reached for the manila folder on her lap with the red top secret coversheet and flipped it open.

"Sir," she said, "we have received confirmation that the Spear of Destiny theft by China has failed, and the original artifact is back in the Hofburg Palace Museum and secure."

Trump leaned back in his chair and looked at the stack of folders flowing out of his *In Box*. He extracted the top one labeled *Timeless Destiny* and flipped it open. The President was always amused at the code names used for operations.

"Mmm," mused President Trump, "uh-huh."

He looked at Metta and asked, "What about Captain Ross? Is he all right? What have we heard from him?"

Braxton Matthews spoke up.

"Sir I can answer that."

President Trump looked over at General Matthews.

Four-star General Braxton Matthews graduated at the top of his class from West Point. He was a career Special Forces officer, with multiple worldwide command and staff tours. Matthews had impressed President Trump so much by his initiatives to eradicate the ISIS caliphate that Trump made him his Army Chief of Staff. His experience with intelligence organizations was that they were interconnected by a surprisingly delicate structure, and loathed interfacing with each other to share information. US intelligence had become an intricate web where one hand didn't know what the other hand was doing. Information was provided too late or not at all. He swore to himself that if ever given the chance he would provide accurate information and as timely as possible.

Matthews said, "If you remember sir, Captain Ross's plane was seen crashing into the Chinese warehouse on Abaco, but AWACS surveillance picked up heat signatures of two people leaving the aircraft, possibly in a gyroplane. We lost track of them over the Triangle."

President Trump looked perplexed.

"Triangle?" asked the President.

Matthews clasped his hands together on his lap. "Ah — the Bermuda Triangle, sir."

Trump steeled his gaze and let out a low whistle. He threw the top secret folder on top of the Resolute desk and leaned back in his chair.

Matthews said, "Sir, I was able to establish communications with Captain Ross. He verified for me that he destroyed the Abaco warehouse to prevent the Chinese from getting hold of Die Glocke, the supposed time machine."

Trump jotted down some notes in the folder.

"And he also verified that he had to kill Admiral Shui Gui in the process. It was a matter of self-defense," said Matthews. "And last week, Captain Ross stopped the Chinese team from stealing the Spear of Destiny."

Trump asked, "So, they were in fact attempting to steal it? Right out of the Hofburg?"

"Yes sir. Absolutely," replied Matthews.

"Sir, do you remember when we briefed you on the World War Two device codenamed Die Glocke, the Bell?"

"Yes, I certainly do," replied President Trump. "The alleged Nazi time machine. Where is it now?"

"Still in Vienna, under Ross's control," replied Matthews.

"Okay," said the President. "Good. We need to arrange to get that into our hands before anything else happens."

"By the way," asked the President, "what happened to the Chinese team?"

General Braxton Matthews looked at the other advisors seated in the Oval Office.

"They're dead sir. All four of them," said Matthews.

"I see," said the President.

Turning his attention to his NSA Director, Trump asked, "What's the latest traffic we're picking up on this, Teresa?"

NSA Director Teresa Cenni was a graduate of the University of Hawaii. A former surfer turned career US Navy Signal Corps officer, she still wore the Bulova surfboard chronograph watch with orange Swiss Tropic strap that her parents had given her for her twenty-fifth birthday. Teresa Cenni was named after her great grandmother, La

Contessa Teresa di Cenni, whose claim to fame was that her husband, Santino, was the first to open a Bugatti dealership in Milan. Teresa had made a name for herself in the satellite and imagery field, and had retired at the rank of Vice Admiral. Shortly thereafter she was appointed by President Trump as his personal choice for NSA Director.

Director Cenni stood up to address the President.

"Please sit and make yourself comfortable, Teresa," said President Trump gesturing to the sofa.

"Look," said the President, "does this Die Glocke, or Bell, or whatever the hell it is actually work? Does it really function? I mean, does the damn thing even exist?"

NSA Director Teresa Cenni tried to reassure the President.

"Yes sir," said Teresa. "It does exist. It is real."

Teresa started to read from the folder in her hands.

"Sir, back in 1944 when the Third Reich was falling apart, SS-Obersturmbannführer Otto Skorzeny had entrusted his colleague, Obersturmführer Wilhelm von Lugoff, to safeguard Die Glocke. Die Glocke was actually designed to open a portal through time itself. It was a type of transporter to the past or the future. Through testing, Die Glocke was found to be able to transfer a man into the fourth dimension. It appears sir, that it *was* a time machine."

President Trump stared intently at his NSA Director.

"Sir, the Nazis planned enormous military applications for Die Glocke. The idea was to transport select troops into the time vortex to conduct military operations that would guarantee total victory and win the war for Germany. A certain General Hans Kammler had been the engineer in charge of the V-2 missiles, and had been personally chosen by Himmler to lead the Nazi time travel project.  It's even believed that his complete disappearance at the end of the war had something to do with the machine.  Some said he transported himself to the future, and then returned the Bell back to the past.  It has been chronicled in a scrub of our classified National Archives files that the Bell was actually responsible for the Kecksburg Pennsylvania UFO incident.  Sir, the following information has all been verified through our high surveillance platforms including RAMPART, PRISM, and MYSTIC, and also with DIA's STONE GHOST.  We currently have eyes on the Nazi time machine right now.  It is resting in a field, two kilometers northeast of the Hofburg Palace Museum, covered by three feet of snow."

Trump thought for a second.

"Okay, and what are we doing to secure it?" asked the President.

Metta Ngernluan looked around the room at her colleagues for comments.  CIA Director Kliner raised her arm.

Anna Kliner was a former military brat. She was the honor graduate in her Air Force ROTC class at Yale University, and received her commission as an Intelligence officer.  She served for over thirty years and retired as a Lieutenant General, with her final assignment being as Director of the Defense Intelligence Agency (DIA) on Joint Base Anacostia-Bolling in Washington DC.  President Trump had been impressed with her intelligence reports proving that the COVID-19 virus was actually specifically engineered and weaponized militarily as a bio-weapon, and that China had deliberately released it through its civilian airline travelers to crash world economies and, hopefully, crash President Trump's reelection bid. China hated Trump's tariffs, trade restrictions, and tough military posturing in the Pacific. They wanted him gone. So it was no surprise to anyone that President Trump appointed Anna as his CIA Director.

"Sir, we have a Diplomatic Security Service team out of our embassy in Vienna alerted to secure the Nazi time machine. However, it turns out the Chinese archeological team sent after the Longinus Spear was not the only team dispatched from the Chinese Ministry of State Security. It appears another team is operating in the area," reported Anna.

"How many teams are there?" asked the President. "Total."

Anna said, "Our own DSS team, at least one more Chinese team, and possibly an Israeli team."

President Trump asked, "Israeli team?"

"Yes sir," said Anna. "A Mossad team."

"How do we know that?" asked the President.

Anna said, "Last week there was an attempt in Zurich to locate a certain Lin Sparrow, who we believe is the girlfriend of Captain James Ross. The Chinese sent a team, and so did Israel. Members of the Chinese team were killed."

President Trump thought for a second. "Why? What happened? What were they after?"

"Die Glocke, sir," said Anna. "We feel that Captain Ross had possession of the sole surviving example of the Nazi time travel mechanism. There was a gunfight between the Chinese and Israeli's. Two of the Chinese were killed."

President Trump tried to take it all in.

"Okay. Keep me informed. Notify me once the Bell is secured," said the President.

General Braxton Matthews stared at the CIA Director. This was information he was hearing for the very first time, otherwise he would have alerted Ross when he had talked with him last week.

"Sir," continued Anna, "we have received reports that this new Chinese team consists of medical personnel, and its primary mission is psychological warfare."

Anna waited for a response from the President.

President Trump picked up a pen from his desk and started writing again inside his *Timeless Destiny* folder. After a few seconds he asked, "Okay, is Ross safe?"

General Matthews replied, "Sir, I tried to contact him this morning but got no response. I'll keep trying again after this meeting."

President Donald Trump studied the four faces of his most trusted staff officers sitting in from of him.

"All right then. We'll be in Vienna for a week. And I want to meet Captain Ross and personally decorate him. He's done his country a great service, and I want to show our gratitude," said Trump.

"Braxton, I want you to monitor this Ross situation very closely. Brief me daily."

"Yes sir," replied General Matthews.

"And Anna, I'm very concerned about this second Chinese team. I want to know everything that is happening with them," said the President.

"Roger that sir."

"All of you coordinate. I want to know everything that is going on with this time-travel device, and I want it secured by our people as soon as possible."

The trusted advisors all nodded simultaneously.

"Keep me informed. Okay, that's it for now," said President Trump.

The four staff officers rose to attention and walked out of the Oval Office.

# CHAPTER FOUR

# MSS

In Beijing China near Tiananmen Square at number 100 Xiyuan Haidian District is located an interesting building complex. It could be the manufacturing hub for Chinese electric car batteries, or perhaps the headquarters of an information technology conglomerate. But it's not any of these. The buildings appear relatively mundane except for the high walls, fences, barbed wire, armed guards, and rooftops festooned with antennas. Named the Yidongyuan Compound, it houses the headquarters for the Chinese Ministry of State Security, or MSS. The MSS is the principal intelligence, national security, and secret police agency in the Communist People's Republic of China. The MSS is one of the world's largest and most secretive intelligence organizations, with multiple branch offices situated throughout China. Their manpower is over 110,000 strong. The motto of the MSS is: "To serve the people firmly and purely, to reassure the Party, to contribute, to be able to fight hard, and to win."

There are currently thousands of Chinese undercover operatives located throughout the United States. All are actively engaging in espionage from the boardroom to the dorm room. For several years, American Democrat Administration policies allowed thousands of Chinese operatives to illegally enter the United States through its wide open southern border. Trained military age operators crossed over illegally and completely unchecked. In 2013 it was even revealed that California Democrat US Senator Dianne Feinstein had presumably unknowingly employed, for over 20 years, a chauffeur who was an agent of the Chinese Ministry of State Security. Was she admonished for that lack of judgment? Absolutely not.

The MSS consists of 18 separate bureaus, broken down into information technology, counterintelligence, human intelligence, cyber warfare, official and non-official cover operations, trade secret acquisitions, intellectual property theft, foreign university influencing, research institute espionage, foreign governmental agency infiltration, and assassinations. Of these, Bureau #18 is located on the 7th floor of building 1206.

There is a very special meeting taking place today in room 23 of Bureau #18. Room 23 is a SCIF. All Top Secret material discussed inside would never leave the room. If something ever went wrong with an operation, the planner would be killed before President Xi Jinping would be embarrassed. That was Chinese Communist Party justice. The accused would be given a "quick trial." What is a "quick trial?" That's a trial immediately the next day, followed by same-day execution. Bureau #18 conducts and manages all clandestine intelligence operations in and against the United States. Bureau #18 also handles assassinations.  This morning, six top executive officers of the MSS sat around a long mahogany table in room 23.  They were discussing a followup to a failed operation.

"Sir, it appears our team leader Nü Jiangshi has failed us in Vienna," said Colonel Bai Weng.  "Her and the other three members of her team are all dead."

General Yanjin Yixin seethed and was visibly irritated.

"The President demands retaliation.  Who were the other members of her team?" asked the General.

Colonel Bai Weng replied, "Ming Chen, Wutu Shen, and Chong Zee."

General Yixin said, "See to it that each of their fathers is given a quick trial."

Colonel Weng explained, "But Nü Jiangshi's father is already dead. She betrayed him and he died in a concentration camp years ago."

"The mother then," said General Yixin impatiently.

Colonel Weng wrote in his note pad.

"Yes sir.  And sir, I have good news.  Our secondary team is engaged and has taken over the operation."

A wry smile crept across General Yixin's face.

"Explain," asked the General.

"Sir," replied Colonel Weng, "their official cover is as medical personnel working in the Vienna General Hospital.  They were immediately given the mission to kidnap Captain Ross and turn him against the Americans.  It is already in progress."

"And ..." prodded the General.

"... what else?"

Colonel Weng said, "And we can still accomplish the mission of finding the killer of Admiral Shui Gui, and have an added bonus of turning that killer, Captain Ross, into our asset."

"Excellent," said the General.

Colonel Weng said, "Along with that sir, once we have Ross brainwashed, we can get him to deliver the Nazi time travel mechanism to us personally."

"Very good indeed," replied General Yixin. "But, refresh my memory about this Captain Ross, please."

Sycophantic smiles beamed across the faces at the table.

"Yes sir," replied Colonel Weng.

"The man our advanced team identified as Admiral Shui Gui's killer is an American officer. Captain, US Army. His name is Ross. James Ross. He is one of their Special Forces assassins. A Green Beret. But there is one thing very curious."

"What's that?"

"We received reports that Captain Ross may be under charges from his superiors."

"Oh yes, I remember you mentioning that before," said the General. "Charges? For what?"

"Ah," said Colonel Weng sheepishly, "supposedly for illegally entering Switzerland with a diplomatic passport while on military leave."

A cynical frown broke out across General Yixin's face as he sat back in his chair.

"Not a chance," he said. "This is not the prior administration. Those years are over. We lost our greatest political pawn. Back then, we had the President and his family in our pockets. Our million dollar payouts for their influence peddling schemes led directly to our country's power ascension over the world. Of course, we also had to release and then control the bio-weapon known as COVID, but that was a relatively simple affair."

Heads around the table were nodding affirmatively.

General Yixin said, "There is no way that the United States military could be so stupid as to place charges on one of their highly trained Special Forces officers. No way. No, that's a ruse. Created to confuse us."

The other five top executive officers at the table all nodded their heads in agreement.

General Yixin said, "Let me remind you …"

*Here comes another lecture,* thought Colonel Weng.

"… that destruction of the traditional American family was necessary. So we started subtly influencing their children in public schools and universities with our indoctrinated teachers. We taught them to hate and disrespect parental authority. Then we moved forward with destroying their traditional culture. Both the major American political parties are corrupt, the Republicans and the Democrats. But we've found over the years much more greed and corruption with the Democrat Party. Their eagerness to remain in power at any costs was an exploitable advantage for us. The American Democrat Political Party came in handy for that purpose. Our psychological operations experts were correct in surmising how easy it would be to manipulate their politicians to submit to our will. After all, they are composed of individuals who are willing to sell out their culture and traditions for mere money. Money attracts them like gypsy moths to a light. And once we had their politicians duped, it was easy to then introduce our agenda. We started with the racism tactic. We turned to their long-gone-centuries-old Civil War, and manipulated them to dismantle hero statues, rename military bases, and basically alienate half of their own country. We managed to get a police defund movement up and running in all Democrat-led states, and even get their legal system to release violent criminals on no-bail initiatives. The open border policy allowed us to infiltrate twenty-one-thousand of our own operators into the United States for future missions, not to mention the other sixteen-million immigrants who entered illegally and are bankrupting their entire infrastructure. Perhaps our greatest coup was being able to tacitly manipulate their own military leaders through their corrupt politicians. This was extremely paramount to our mission success. We relied on their inherent narcissism. Remember when we brokered the deal to introduce Diversity-Equity-Inclusion training into the American military? We even coerced them to initiate Critical Race Theory at West Point. DEI and CRT are pure Marxist ideology. It wasn't long before we had their own Chairman of the Joint Chiefs telling Congress that he wanted to learn what 'white rage' was."

A cynical smile crept across General Yixin's face.

The other Chinese officers sitting around the table nodded enthusiastically.

"We even had him apologizing to their entire military for walking to a Christian church with their President holding a bible. When we could destroy their history, culture, traditions, family, and religion, we knew we would win.  Remember when we financially supported youthful radicals to organize race riots on their own streets?  We were even able to influence some to deface the sacred Alamo shrine in Texas.  How surprised the Americans seemed when the leaders of those organizations turned out to be mere money-hungry charlatans.  Our 'Woke' program was pure communist theory straight out of the Marxist-Leninist Handbook.  The intent was to divide the United States through manipulating social and mainstream media with deliberate lies.  Divide and conquer — a tactic as old as time.  It was utter nonsense infused into America by us.  We manipulated half their country to hate the other half.  We sought to create division and put into power those politicians who were monetarily beholden to us.  The United States was ready for a complete communist takeover.  Unfortunately, most of our endeavors were dissolved by President Donald Trump once he was elected."

General Yixin looked around the table at his comrades.

"I find it hard to believe that the United States Army would discipline a Green Beret officer — one of their very best — because of misusing a passport," he chuckled.

The other five officers around the table looked at each other and automatically nodded their heads approvingly.

"Yes sir," said Lieutenant Colonel Bohai Xu.  "There is no way the Americans would be that stupid."

General Yixin leaned forward and poured himself a glass of ice cold water from the carafe.  He looked around the table once again at his comrades while taking a sip.  Then he unblinkingly pounded the table with his fist, startling the other officers.

"Just be sure we completely turn this man Ross into our willing asset," said General Yixin.  "President Xi Jinping is counting on it. And we don't want to disappoint the President do we?"

"No sir," replied Colonel Weng.  "Absolutely not."

"By the way," asked the General, "what are your thoughts on a mission for this man Ross once he is brainwashed?"

Colonel Weng said, "The team leader, Doctor Wu Qiang, who is a mind control graduate of the Pavlov Institute and a trained psychiatrist, says the best scenario for Captain Ross, after he delivers us Die Glocke of course,  would be as an assassin."

General Yixin thought for a moment.

"That's very good.  Very good indeed.  We can turn this man around on his own country and give them a chill they'll never forget."

General Yixin stared at the faces around the table.

"Yes sir!" said the other five officers in unison.

# CHAPTER FIVE

# WARLOCK

Doctor Wu Qiang earned his medical degree from Nanjing Medical University.  He attended on a military scholarship and graduated as a Shàngwèi, or Captain, in the People's Liberation Army.  He furthered his education with a fellowship in psychiatry at Moscow's prestigious Pavlov Institute.  There he studied diseases of the mind, and became an expert in psychotherapy and mind control medicines.

Wu was thirty-seven years old, five-feet-nine-inches tall, and weighed a hundred and sixty-five pounds.  His jet black hair was cut short and always parted in the middle.  Wu had a handsome face, except for a strange skin discoloration on the right cheek.  It was caused from a Wuhan lab leak of an experimental incapacitating agent he had been testing for the military.  It left a three-inch-wide spiderweb-looking blackened scar on his face.  Wu kept in shape by practicing Chinese Changquan.  Otherwise known as *Long Fist,* it was a very aggressive martial art from northern China, famous for fully extended kicks and  lightning-fast striking techniques.  The Long Fist motto was: "The best defense is a strong offense."

At the Pavlov Institute, Wu studied the whole gauntlet of serotonin and norepinephrine uptake inhibitors, the tricyclics, and of course the dreaded scopolamine.   Known on the street as *Devil's Breath,* scopolamine is derived from the Columbian borrachero tree.  Use of scopolamine can lead to the patient losing their free will, along with amnesia.   The patient literally becomes a zombie that can be fully controlled.

Doctor Wu Qiang was known to his MSS colleagues as *Warlock. Wu* in Mandarin stands for sorcerer or warlock, and *Qiang* means powerful.  Many of his colleagues were terrified of him because of his ruthlessness and zeal.


Ross had been transferred from emergency room three to the twelfth floor.   There he was sequestered into a private room and heavily sedated with intravenous propofol.  Doctor Wu's plan was to use a combination of psychotherapy and scopolamine to brainwash Ross.

"The patient must remain sedated," explained Doctor Wu to his three colleagues, "since a man of Captain Ross's physical strength and mental resilience will resist us, even unconsciously."

Surrounding Ross's hospital bed were Zao Konton, Boi Kyuki, and Mei Fang.   All three were young highly trained counterintelligence agents.  Doctor Wu considered them his Xian's, or *Immortals.*

Zao Konton asked, "How long does it take the drug to be effective, sir?"

"It starts working in four hours, but is most effective after eight or twelve hours," replied Doctor Wu.

Boi Kyuki said, "This man Ross, do you feel his former training in Special Forces will subconsciously increase his resistance, his willpower? I have heard these American Special Forces men have highly disciplined minds and are extremely resilient. I mean, look at his body. He is lean and muscled. He looks formidable. He looks like a piece of iron."

Twenty-four-year-old Mei Fang had indeed been looking at James Ross's body. As the only female member of the team, she still remained single. She loathed dating Chinese soldiers, especially officers, as they dated purely for communist political reasons and personal gain. Although a devoted communist, Mei still believed in love, and was secretly reading a smuggled copy of *The Time Traveler's Wife* by Audrey Niffenegger. The concept of freedom always intrigued her, and she sometimes privately questioned her own loyalty to the State. She was petite at five-feet-two-inches tall, and weighed a hundred and ten pounds. Mei was very attractive with or without makeup, physically fit, and she wore her silky black hair in a Western pixie cut.

Mei stared at Ross's face.

*He's very handsome,* she thought. *He must be Amerasian. It's a very strong face. A beautiful, handsome, strong face.*

She looked at his dark brown hair, now matted with sweat, and hanging in disarray about his face.

*What must it feel like to run your fingers through that hair?* she pondered.

Then she stared at his body.

Mei pointed with her finger.

"What kinds of wounds are they, sir?  Are those bullet wounds?" she asked.

Doctor Wu leaned over Ross and took a look.

"Yes, as a matter of fact they are," he said.

Wu started to gently probe Ross's body with his hands.

"It appears he has a bullet wound in the right shoulder here just above the clavicle, and another one in his right leg, and yet another halfway up on his right side here at the ribcage.  Do you see?"

"Yes," replied Mei.

Then Wu pointed with his finger.

"You see those smaller wounds, the smaller scars?"

Mei leaned over and looked at Ross closer.

"Yes," she said.

"Those are shrapnel wounds," said Wu.  "Captain Ross most probably received them from coming in contact with grenades or some other explosives."

*So many scars,* Mei thought. *Too many for one so young.*

Then she wondered who this man was in the club with when he was drugged?  She wondered if it was a girl, and if she was Ross's girlfriend?  She wondered how it would be to love a man like Captain James Ross?

Doctor Wu Qiang noticed his young female assistant's affectionate staring at Ross.

Wu said, "What do you think, comrade Fang?"

Mei measured her words carefully.

"This American soldier will be an interesting challenge and a great coup for the People's Republic."

# CHAPTER SIX

# A FRIEND

Lin inquired about Ross at the hospital information desk.

"Mademoiselle, may I help you?" asked the receptionist.

"Yes, please. My fiancé James Ross was brought in at two o'clock in the morning today. He was taken to the emergency room. I've been in the waiting room since then. I'd like to find out his status."

"Didn't they let you know his status in the waiting room?" asked the receptionist.

"No. No one came. I haven't been told anything. I haven't been given any update," answered Lin.

The receptionist had a puzzled look on her face. "Let me see what's going on," she said as she punched numbers into the phone in front of her.

"Hello ER? This is Elizabeth at the information desk. Can you please give me a status update on a James Ross? Yes, that's right, James Ross."

Lin stared intently at the receptionist.

"What's that?  Oh, okay.  Do you have an address?" asked the receptionist as she picked up a pen and stared writing on a notepad.

*Address?* thought Lin.  *What in the world?*

"Okay, thank you, thank you."

The receptionist hung up the phone.  She tore the page off her notepad and gave it to Lin.

"He's being transferred to a private clinic," said the receptionist.  "Something to do with his health insurance."

"What?" exclaimed Lin.  "That doesn't make any sense."

The receptionist shook her head.

"I'm sorry, but here's the address.  That's where he is, or at least where he will be."

Lin asked, "When was he transferred?"

The receptionist shrugged her shoulders.

"Looks like it might be happening right now."

"Where?" asked Lin frantically.

The receptionist pointed with her finger.

"Outside, to the right," she said.

Lin ran to the exit and impatiently waited for the double glass doors to electronically slide open.  Then she went through and quickly turned the corner and sprinted to where the ambulances were parked.  She saw an ambulance pull away from the hospital with siren blaring and lights flashing.  Lin realized she would never be able to catch it.

*This is nuts,* thought Lin.

She looked at the address in her hands.

*The only thing to do is take a taxi to this private care facility.*

Lin Sparrow walked out to Währinger Gürtel Strasse and yelled, "Taxi!"

In ten seconds a gray Mercedes-Benz sedan pulled up to her.

"Where to, mademoiselle?" asked the driver.

Lin showed him the address.

"Very well," said the driver, "Reitschulgasse twenty-three."

Lin stepped into the taxi and it sped away.

They passed Freyung square, which is famous for hosting the Altwiener Christkindlmarkt, and then they drove up Teinfaltstrabe and past the huge Rathausplatz market.

In about fifteen minutes they reached their destination.

"Here you are mademoiselle, number 23 Reitschulgasse," said the driver as he expertly pulled the Mercedes to a stop directly in front.

She paid the driver and the taxi left quickly.

Lin stood in front of the facility and read the name on its bronze overhead placard.

*Healing Minds Center.*

Suddenly she felt a shudder.

She walked to the entrance and the double paned glass doors automatically hissed open. The information desk was located just to the left as she hurried inside. A young Chinese man greeted her.

"How may I help you?" politely asked the information desk attendant. On his nametag was printed *Yeung*.

"Yes, thank you," said Lin. "My fiancé was just brought in here. His name is James Ross."

Yeung picked up the desk phone and said, "Let me check." He punched in some numbers and spoke very softly.

"Yes hello, this is Yeung at the front desk.  Did we just admit a Mister James Ross?  Yes that's right.  What?  Okay, I'll see," said Yeung.

He clasped his hand over the phone receiver and asked Lin, "They want to know who is asking, please?"

Lin answered, "I'm Lin Sparrow.  I'm his fiancée."

Yeung spoke again very softly into the phone.

"His fiancée is here, a Mademoiselle Lin Sparrow," said Yeung.

The response came, and suddenly a quizzical look overtook Yeung's face.

"What's that?  Really?  Is that something new?  Oh okay.  Yes.  All right.  Thanks.  Bye."

Yeung's expression became crestfallen.

"I'm very sorry Mademoiselle Sparrow, but they say James Ross is here, but I can not allow you to see him because you are not a relative."

"What?" exclaimed Lin.  "That's not right!  I'm his fiancée!"

Yeung looked at her with sad eyes.

"I know, I know.  I understand.  But unfortunately that's the way it is.  I'm sorry."

"But, I need to see him.  I need to know what's happening.  How is he?  Is he recovering?  How long will he be here?  What's happening?" asked Lin.

Yeung gave her his sad eyes again.

"I understand.  I really do.  And I'm very sorry," he said.

Lin stepped back from the front desk and took in the entire scene. Every detail of the reception area became imprinted on her brain.  The stairs, the elevators, the hallways, and especially that she did not see a security guard.  She was going to remember it all.

"Can you at least tell me what floor and room he's in?" asked Lin.

Yeung suddenly felt very sorry for her and leaned forward.  He looked  around a couple times and motioned for her to come closer.

"He's on the second floor, in room 212," he whispered.

Lin smiled and reached out touching his hand and said, "Thank you sincerely."  Then she turned around and walked out of the building.

Large flakes of glistening late December snow were gently wafting down outside.  Lin suddenly noticed the cold.  Her body was starting to come down off of its adrenaline high that it had been on for the past couple hours.  Lin was still dressed in her bluejeans, sneakers, and blue sweater from the night before.  She pulled up the collar of Ross's red wool jacket against the cold.  The playful snowflakes encircled her, and merged with the rest of the frosty winter wonderland at her feet.

*I need someone's help with this,* thought Lin.  *But who?  Who do I know that can possibly help me?*

There was only one choice.

"Inus," she said to herself.  "Lon G. Inus."

A few days ago Lon Inus had given Ross his business card, and Ross had given it to Lin.  She pulled out her iPhone and scrolled up his cellphone number.


Lon G. Inus was in his apartment on Mariahilfer Strasse.  He had been up since dawn and was planning on visiting the Hofburg Palace Museum.  He visited it daily.  It was his sole routine.  He stood for hours looking at the Longinus Spear. Also known as the Spear of Destiny and the Holy Lance, it was said to have mystical powers. Some claimed it was able to heal the sick, bring victory in battles, and even foretell the future.

Some considered Lon G. Inus to be handsome. Sporting classic good looks, he was thirty-four years old, six-foot-two, 187 pounds, had shiny black hair always cut short, suntanned, and was extremely fit. The letters *SPQR* were tattooed on his left forearm. Most people thought he was Italian. Inus always dressed conservatively in a black suit with long black overcoat. At a distance he looked like a young Sylvester Stallone. There was one thing about him that some women found most endearing — his dark brown eyes — they looked sad.

*Why did it have to be me?* Longinus asked himself for the millionth time.

*Why did I have to pick up that spear?*

*Why?*

He shook his head.

*Jesus was already dead.*

*I thought I was giving him peace.*

Then the regret came once again.

*Why didn't I stop it?*

*Why didn't I speak up?*

*Why couldn't I have let it all alone?*

Longinus took a moment to remember. He had buried his wife and daughters centuries ago. He had watched everyone he ever loved pass away. Through the two millennia he had already lived since that tragic day, the Centurian known as Longinus had come to realize that he was kept alive to protect the Spear of Destiny. His task was to safeguard the spear until the return of Jesus Christ.

*If only I could have left it alone.*

Longinus sat in a cushioned chair and opened his bible. This bible contained the Apocryphal Gospels. Longinus turned to the Gospel of Nicodemus and began to read aloud in Greek.

"Then Longinus, a certain soldier, taking a spear, pierced his side, and …"

*Cursed,* he thought.

*Cursed to remain until the return of the man I killed.*

*But I didn't kill him, did I?*

*No. No I didn't kill him.*

*Jesus was destined to die.*

*Jesus was sent here to die.*

*Jesus Christ died to set all men free.*

*He died for love.*

Then Longinus turned to John 15:13 and read aloud.

"There is no greater love than this, that a man lay down his life for his friends."

Longinus closed his bible and took his face in his hands. He began to weep.

*Brrring!*

*Brrring!*

*Brrring!*

Longinus picked up his cellphone and saw it was Lin Sparrow calling.

"Hello Lin. What a pleasant surprise," said Longinus.

Lin frantically cried, "Oh thank God!  Lon, I really need your help! You're the only one I can trust!"

Longinus immediately snapped out of his depression.

"Okay, okay Lin, slow down.  What is it?  What's going on?" he asked.

Lin rapidly said, "I think James has been kidnapped by the Chinese, and I can't see him, and they have him at someplace called the Healing Minds Center at Reitschulgasse 23."

Longinus sat up in his chair.

He said, "Okay, okay Lin.  When did all this happen?"

Lin started to calm down and replied, "Just after you left us last night. We stayed in the lounge to dance a little and had some champagne.  The champagne was drugged because James passed out and we had to call for an ambulance."

"Go on," said Longinus.

"So, the ambulance took him to Vienna General Hospital, and at the hospital four Chinese medics were waiting for him …"

Longinus knew it would be exceedingly rare to find four Chinese medical personnel at Vienna General.

"… and then told me to wait in the waiting room, which I did, and they never came back to give me any information.  Then I was told they transferred him to the Healing Minds Center."

"What happened after that?" asked Longinus.

Lin said, "Then I went over to the place and found out he was admitted but they wouldn't let me see him because they said I wasn't a relative.  And I told them James is my fiancé, but they still wouldn't let me see him."

"Where are you now, Lin?" asked Longinus.

"I'm standing outside the Healing Minds Center," she replied.

Longinus said, "Okay. Get a taxi and go back to your hotel. I'll meet you in your room in twenty minutes, all right?"

Lin said, "Yes, all right, and thank you so much Lon."

"Try not to worry. We'll figure out what to do and come up with a plan," said Longinus reassuringly.

Lin asked, "Lon, do you think this is another Chinese intelligence team?"

That was indeed what he thought.

Longinus said, "I'll knock on your door in twenty minutes."

Then he ended the call.

# PART TWO

*Out of every hundred men, ten shouldn't even be there, eighty are just targets, nine are the real fighters, and we are lucky to have them, for they make the battle.  Ah, but the one, one is a warrior, and he will bring the others back.*

Heraclitus
500 BC
Greek Philosopher

# CHAPTER SEVEN

# WHERE AM I?

*I'm floating.*

*Seems like I'm floating outside my body.*

*I'm floating beside my body.*

*It's snowing.*

*I'm in a field of white snow.*

*I can see Die Glocke.*

*There's a group of people.*

*There's shooting.*

*People are fighting around Die Glocke.*

*There's an explosion.*

*Now there's only darkness.*

*I'm in a graveyard.*

*A rain soaked, misty graveyard.*

*I see Lin.*

*She's walking towards me.*

*Lin's crying.*

*Why are you crying?*

*She's bending down.*

*She's placing a wreath on a grave.*

*It's my grave!*

*Now she collapses and pounds the freshly dug earth with her fists.*


Ross's eyes fluttered open.

*Where am I?* he thought.

He gazed around the room.

*Looks like I'm in a hospital room of some sort,* he thought.

He struggled to get up, but found he was physically strapped to a hospital bed.

"What the hell?" he said.

There were two intravenous infusion bags hanging on a pole next to the bed. Ross saw IV tubing from the bags running to a catheter in his left arm. Whatever was in the bags was dripping into him.

"Christ," said Ross.

He struggled again against his bonds.

The door to the room suddenly opened and in walked a man.

*Looks Chinese,* thought Ross.

Doctor Wu Qiang walked over to Ross.

"Good morning Captain Ross," Wu said. "And how are you feeling today?"

Ross said, "Where am I? What happened? How long have I been here? Who are you?"

Wu smiled his bad-teeth smile.

"My goodness!  So many questions.  But I guess you deserve some answers.  My name is Wu Qiang — Doctor Wu Qiang.  You are my patient."

Ross struggled against his restraints.

"Now, now, Captain Ross," admonished Wu.  "You must remain absolutely calm before we can release you back into polite society.  Let me try to answer your questions.  Let's see, what happened is that we drugged you in the lounge of the Herrenhof Steigenberger Hotel.  It was a simple matter using a date-rape drug named flunitrazepam.  The effect was exacerbated by the alcohol in your glass.  As to where you are, that's easy.  You are still in Vienna, at the Healing Minds Center.  And because of your rebellious nature, you are receiving psychiatric care.  And we only just received you last night."

Ross said, "What the hell is this all about?"

Wu nodded his head.  "I suppose that is really the only question, isn't it?"

Wu moved a chair to the side of the bed and sat down next to Ross.

"Did you think there was only one team?" he asked.  "Did you believe that the people you killed were all there was?  No, not at all.  You may have stopped some of us, but we are a patient people, Captain Ross.  We have time on our side.  We can wait for as long as it takes."

Ross said, "As long as it takes for what?"

"To bury your pathetic country under the dung heap of history," said Wu.  "You see, you are about to become a soldier of the People's Liberation Army.  You are about to become a very valuable asset."

Ross said, "You're crazy."

"On the contrary Captain Ross, I am amazingly sane," said Wu.

"Do you see the IV hanging next to you?"

Ross turned his head and looked.

"Yeah I see it," said Ross.

Wu explained, "The large bag is just normal saline, used as a diluting agent. But the smaller bag is filled with scopolamine. Do you know what that is?"

Ross flippantly said, "A new diet cola?"

Wu smarted and said, "Ah yes, the famous American sense of humor. I will have to learn to get used to that."

Ross said, "Go ahead, explain it why don't you?"

Wu said, "Scopolamine is derived from the Columbian borrachero tree. It's from the antimuscarinic family of drugs, and is an acetylcholine blocking agent. It's used effectively in anesthesia, however, it also has very strong psychoactive properties, mainly hallucinogenic and amnesic. Effective use of scopolamine therapy can lead to the patient losing their free will, along with amnesia. In other words, the patient literally becomes a zombie that can be fully controlled."

Ross struggled again against his bonds.

Wu explained, "We decided not to kill you, but to use you. You see, can you imagine the astonished looks on your superiors faces when we send you back to spy for us or blow up something? What a propaganda coup that will be."

Ross said, "It won't work. You'll be stopped."

Wu asked, "But by who? Who will stop us Captain Ross?"

Ross answered, "The United States, that's who."

Wu said, "Our goal is to discredit the United States in the eyes of the world.   Perhaps we will even send you to assassinate someone? Your superior?  Maybe your President?  After all, with your skill set, it will literally be just like deploying a cruise missile."

*Jesus Christ,* thought Ross.  *What kind of a nightmare is this?*

# CHAPTER EIGHT

# MOSSAD

Lin had used the Nazi time machine to escape the gun battle which had erupted last week at the Asiatisches Essen Philippine Restaurant in Zurich. That was where she and Ross had been staying at the behest of their old friend, Emanuel Mesiyas. Emanuel was the enigmatic Philippine taxicab driver who had shared many of their past adventures.

It was through Emanuel that Ross was introduced to Mossad.

*Mossad* is a Hebrew word, translated into English as "The Institute." Their entire title is "The Institute for Intelligence and Special Operations." Mossad is the national intelligence agency of Israel, much like the CIA is for the United States. Mossad's primary missions include: counterterrorism, intelligence collection, and operations. Mossad reports directly to the Prime Minister of Israel. The Mossad team Ross had been introduced to had been operating out of the Israeli consulate in Zurich. The men were all friends of

Emanuel — Yitzhak Zanir, Shabtai Yatom, Benjamin Shiloah, and Zvi Harel. They were always well-groomed and dressed in dark suits. They were all in their late twenties, extremely fit, and with hair slightly longer than that normally found on soldiers. Yitzhak Zanir was the youngest of the men, and was the Kidon commissioned team leader. The restaurant gun battle had resulted in the deaths of two out of three members of a rival Chinese intelligence team sent to obtain Die Glocke. The Mossad men had killed them.

It had taken several days for Israeli intelligence to figure out just exactly where Lin had gone. Their cyber intelligence teams isolated her phone calls and hacked into the Hofburg Palace communications mainframe. The information they intercepted revealed the attempt to steal the Spear of Destiny, and the deaths of the members of the Chinese Archaeology Team. Once the information had been obtained, they immediately flew to Vienna.

A blustery burst of frigid December air sprinkled with snowflakes swirled through the entranceway of the Herrenhof Steigenberger Hotel as four men hurried inside. The men were the Mossad team.

Outside, Longinus pulled his black Audi A5 Cabriolet to the valet station of the Herrenhof Steigenberger Hotel. The young valet took his keys and gave him a ticket. Longinus took it and then sprinted up the front steps of the Steigenberger.

Once inside, Longinus immediately noticed the four men gathered at the front reception desk.

*They're certainly not Chinese. They look Middle Eastern. They must be the Mossad team,* he thought.

Longinus knew Lin was on the third floor in room 323.

He hurried to the elevator.

No sooner were the elevator doors closing than one of the Mossad men stuck his foot between the sliding doors.

"Pardon me sir.  Going up?" Yitzhak said politely.

Longinus pressed the button to open the elevator doors and the Mossad team entered.

"Yes, sorry," said Longinus.

Longinus moved to the left rear of the elevator so as not to allow the Mossad men to surround him.

Yitzhak saw that the third floor button was already pressed and just politely stood with folded hands staring at the blinking display panel.

The ride to the third floor was humorously quiet.

Then the doors slid open and they all got out and walked down the hall.  The Mossad men stopped in front of room 323.

"I'm sorry," said Longinus, "but that's my room."

Yitzhak turned and looked at Longinus.

"We're told that our colleague is waiting for us in this room," said Shabtai.

Longinus reached into his overcoat pocket and grasped the Italian Rizzuto stiletto he always carried.

"I'm afraid you've been given wrong information.  You see, only my wife is in this room, waiting for me.  We've been on vacation for the past week.  So you see, you've made a mistake," said Longinus.

Yitzhak smiled politely.

"Yes, it certainly appears we have.  Sorry about that," said Yitzhak.

The Mossad men turned and slowly followed their team leader back to the elevator.

As soon as the team was gone, Longinus knocked three times on the door of room 323.

Inside, Lin Sparrow peeked through the security door viewer. She saw it was Longinus and opened the door.

"Come in Lon, come in," said Lin. "Thank God you're here."

# CHAPTER NINE

# BRAINWASHING

Doctor Wu Qiang was monitoring Ross's vital signs and reading the results to his assistant Boi Kyuki, who was then inputting them into a bedside laptop computer.

"Blood pressure 118 over 78, heart rate 58, respirations 12, temperature 97.9," said Wu.

The scopolamine drug was infusing into Ross. Wu had also attached electrodes to Ross's forehead which were stimulating the hemispheres. The right hemisphere associates with imagination, emotion, and creativity, while the left hemisphere focuses on language, logic, and critical thinking. Wu was utilizing a form of trans-cranial direct current stimulation which had been invented by Russian scientist Ivan Pavlov in the early twentieth century. Headphones were attached to Ross which had the same propaganda messages repeating over and over. Zao Konton stood by Doctor Wu and was filming the entire scene.

"How much longer will the therapy be applied for today, sir?" asked Zao.

Wu looked at his Apple watch.

"I'll stop the infusion in thirty minutes, but the trans-cranial stimulation and psychotherapy will continue for three more hours," said Wu.

Ross was fighting the therapy.

Although he was physically restrained to the bed, he struggled to dig his fingernails into his palms with balled fists.

*Concentrate your mind on the pain,* remembered Ross from his Fort Bragg Survival Evasion Resistance and Escape (SERE) training.

But soon the assistant who was filming the procedures, Zao, noticed what Ross was doing.

"Doctor Qiang, the American is attempting to overcome the effects of your treatment through self-induced pain," said Zao. "Notice his hands."

Wu looked down and saw Ross's clenched fists.

"Hmm. Yes I see," said Wu.

Wu went to his medical crash cart and took out two rolls of Coban gauze. He placed one each in Ross's palms and then taped up Ross's hands around them.

"There you are my dear Captain Ross," said Wu. "We can't have you distracting from the therapy now can we? Yes sir, no more Green Beret tricks today. As a matter of fact …"

Wu went back to the crash cart and took out a plastic dental guard bite plate. He walked over to Ross and was attempting to force it into Ross's mouth when Ross viciously bit down on Wu's fingers.

"Aiiieeeeeeee!" screamed Wu.

"Help me!  Help me!"

Zao and Boi dropped everything and ran over to Wu.  Zao pushed his hands down on Ross's forehead and Boi pried open Ross's jaw. Wu extracted his fingers, but not before blood started to ooze out of the wounds.

"The American is an animal!" cried Wu.

With Zao's assistance, Boi forced open Ross's jaw and placed the plastic bite guard around his teeth.

Mei Fang heard the doctor's scream and went into the room.

"What has happened?" Mei asked.

She saw Doctor Qiang wrapping a bandage around his fingers.

"Ah, just a slight accident comrade, that's all," said Wu.  "Nothing to concern yourself with."

Wu finished bandaging his hand and said, "Whatever you do, don't turn your back on the American."

The three members of the Chinese team looked at Wu.

"And that goes for the rest of you.  This man Ross is dangerous, but we will take the sting out of him.  By the time I'm done ..." said Wu walking over to Mei, "... he will have no will of his own.  He will become the perfect tool of the People's Liberation Army."

Wu said, "Get me a syringe with midazolam."

Zao went to the medical cart and brought the syringe to Doctor Qiang.

Wu motioned with his head.  "Inject it into his IV port," ordered Wu.

Zao did as he was told.

Within a few seconds Ross fell into a deep sleep.

Wu walked to the medical cart and extracted a surgical incision kit.

"The time has come for the implant," said Wu.

Zao and Boi nodded in agreement.

Wu unfolded a light blue chux pad at bedside and looked at Ross's right forearm. He motioned for Zao and Boi to help him.

"Hold down his right arm," ordered Wu.

Zao and Boi steadied Ross's arm while Wu, despite getting the painful bite from Ross, made a tiny incision with a Grafix scalpel.

"The incision does not need to be deep to accommodate the implant," explained Wu. Then he used forceps to pick up a tiny oblong plastic tube.

"This will time-release scopolamine into his bloodstream. Our research has shown it should last for two weeks. I'm using this as a backup to the pills which I will send Captain Ross home with. Pills which appear to be simple electrolyte replenishers, but are in fact scopolamine themselves." Then Wu slid the implant under Ross's skin and carefully sutured shut the incision. He placed a small bandage over the site.

"The patient will be perfectly primed and receptible to receive the activation codeword by phone call or text message. Once the codeword is given, he will stop at nothing to complete his mission," explained Wu.

Mei turned and looked at Ross.

*What am I doing here?* thought Mei. *I hate what I'm doing, and I hate these people. But I've got no choice. I've got to play this game to protect my parents in Chengdu.*

"Do you need anything else, Doctor?" asked Mei.

Wu shook his head.

"No, that's all.  Captain Ross will wake up in about fifteen minutes.  He may still try to resist, but it will become more and more futile.  Keep monitoring his vital signs.  I'll return in a few hours." Then Doctor Wu left the room.

Mei stood by Ross's bed and looked at his face.  She wondered what kind of friend he would have been if she'd have known him.

*Probably a good one,* she thought.


Ross awoke in fifteen minutes.

He stared around the room through blurred vision and saw that it was empty.

He had a severe headache and felt confused.

*Think damn it, think.*

Ross started to meditate.

He concentrated on his breathing and slowed it down.

Then he cleared his mind of all thoughts.

He imagined taking a broom and sweeping out every thought, no matter what it was.

Next, he introduced an image of the one thing that could save him — an image of Lin Sparrow.

Ross concentrated on Lin.

He imagined her walking on a beach.

She was walking towards him and smiling.

Ross focused his mind on the image of Lin.

He imagined himself as a sponge soaking her in.

The mind control therapy was having its affect however. He could feel himself slipping over the edge. The combination of the sopolamine drug infusing, trans-cranial treatment with electrodes on his forehead, and the constant bombardment of propaganda through the headphones was distracting him, and making it harder to meditate. The messages pumping through the headphones consisted of anti-American propaganda about how terrible the United States was, and how the government was colonial and filled with capitalist corruption. There were messages about how America was a racist country in the past, and continues to be racist. Messages followed about America losing its values, history, and culture. A narrative was being replayed over and over of America being an aggressor nation. Messages also followed with how wonderful Communism was, and how benevolent the People's Republic of China was. There were also messages about the wonderful leadership of President Xi Jinping, and how loyal Communist Party members must devote their entire lives, bodies, and minds to the Leader, and be willing to die for the State.

Ross thought to himself, *Come on, come on, fight it. Think of Lin. Think of Lin. Think ... of ... Lin ...*

Then Ross's eyes became heavy, very heavy.

*Fight,* thought Ross. *Fight.*

His concentration was waning.

*Fight ...*

Finally his eyes closed, but he was still thinking.

*Come on ... fight ...*

Then slowly, unexpectedly, like a gently breeze in the night, he succumbed.

Captain James Ross slowly fell prey to his captors therapy, and lapsed once again into unconsciousness.

# CHAPTER TEN

# THE PLAN

Longinus and Lin were sitting in chairs opposite each other in Ross's hotel room on the third floor of the Herrenhof Steigenberger Hotel. Longinus was trying to digest everything that Lin was saying.

"So, it happened right downstairs, early this morning?" Longinus asked.

"Yes," explained Lin. "Only his champagne glass was laced with flunitrazepam."

"Not yours too?" asked Longinus.

"No, only his," she answered. "They had to have been watching us. The four medical people waiting for him at Vienna General Hospital were speaking Mandarin. They were all Chinese. Three men and one woman. The leader's name is Doctor Wu Qiang."

"How do you know that?" asked Longinus.

"Because I read it on his name tag," she said.

Longinus thought for a second.

"It's definitely a backup team. That's how Chinese intelligence operates. They use backups. There may even be a third team," he said.

Lin shuddered. "I need your help to get James back."

Longinus looked at Lin with his sad eyes.

"You have it, Lin. We will get him back," said Longinus. "I'm going to need you to trust me."

"I do," said Lin.

"Do you have a drink of water?" asked Longinus.

"Oh my goodness, of course I do. Just sit, let me get you something," said Lin apologetically.

Lin stood up and went to the refrigerator. She came back and handed Longinus a cold bottle of water.

"Thank you," said Longinus. "As I see it, our plan must have two tasks. The first is to free James from the Healing Minds Center, and the second is to secure Die Glocke and get you and James back in it and away from here."

Lin nodded.

"They told you no one could see James except a relative, so I'll pretend to be his brother and should be able to visit. What do you think?"

Lin nodded and said, "Okay, it could work."

"I will need some basic information on James in case they challenge me. I already know he's a soldier in the United States Army, and a good shot," he said ironically, "but I'll need to know some personal details such as where he was born and when. Just tell me all you know of him."

Lin started talking and filled in Longinus with the details only she knew of her fiancé James Ross.  He listened intently and committed it all to memory.

"Now, what is the status of Die Glocke?" asked Longinus.

Lin said, "It's in that field over by the Mozart statue, covered with snow."

Longinus nodded his head and said, "I see. That buys us some time, because it's still snowing and the weather doesn't look like it will let up for the next week.  But there's another issue we must deal with."

"What is that?" asked Lin.

Longinus leaned forward in his chair and looked directly into her eyes.

"There were four men which I just intercepted coming into the hotel, and obviously looking for you and James, as they were on their way to your room until I persuaded them it was a mistake."

Lin sat back startled.

"What did they look like?" asked Lin.

Longinus said, "They looked," and Longinus tried to pick his words very carefully because of his background, "they looked like Jews."

Lin said, "Of course, the Israelis."

A puzzled look crept across the face of Longinus.

"The Mossad team.  They must have followed me here," explained Lin.  "They're after Die Glocke as well, just like the Chinese.  Last week in Zurich, the Mossad and Chinese men fought each other over Die Glocke at the place where I was staying."

Longinus put all the pieces of the puzzle together now.

*Everybody wants this damned machine,* he thought.

Lin said, "But nobody can use Die Glocke without this." She showed Longinus the SS dagger. "This is what James was using as a shifter lever after the original one broke. Nobody can travel in Die Glocke without this."

"Oh yeah," said Longinus. "I remember."

Longinus stood up and started pacing about.

"Lin, have you got a gun?" asked Longinus.

Lin walked over to the closet where her jacket was hanging and pulled out Ross's Beretta model 71 pistol in .22LR.

"I've got this," she said showing Longinus the pistol. "I took it out of James' coat pocket before the ambulance picked him up."

"Good," said Longinus, "and I've still got the Chinese pistol. So we should be okay there." The pistol was the Weisheng Shouqiang (QSW-06) suppressed semiautomatic in 5.8x21mm caliber. Ross had taken it off of the Chinese assassin who had attacked them in their room.

Lin walked back and flopped down in the chair.

Longinus asked, "Lin, when was the last time you slept?"

"I'm okay, really. I slept a few hours last night in the waiting room. What do you think we should do next?" she asked.

Longinus said, "Die Glocke is covered with snow and the Mossad team will never find it. So, I need to get over to the Healing Minds Center and see what's going on."

Lin asked, "What do you want me to do, Lon?"

Longinus could see that Lin was almost ready to collapse. He knew she needed some rest.

Longinus said, "I recommend you don't wait here. The Mossad team will likely try and come back. No. You'd better come and stay in my apartment. Gather what you need and come on."

Lin replied, "Okay, give me just a minute."

Since Lin had arrived in Die Glocke with only the clothes on her back, she was ready quickly. She put on Ross's red wool jacket and placed the SS dagger in one pocket and the Beretta pistol in the other. Then she walked into the bathroom and took Ross's toothbrush, toothpaste, and a comb.

"Let's go," she said.

Longinus got up and peeked through the door security viewer first. Seeing no one, he carefully opened the door and peered down both sides of the hallway.

*Nobody,* he thought.

"Okay," said Longinus.

Lin followed him to the elevator and they rode it down to the lobby. Longinus walked with Lin outside to the valet parking. He presented the blue ticket to the young valet.

The young man said, "Yes sir, right away."

He grabbed the ticket and sprinted into the garage. In two minutes the Audi A5 Cabriolet was screeching to a halt in front of the valet station.

"Here you are sir," said the young valet handing Longinus his keys.

The valet opened the doors for Longinus and Lin. Once inside, Longinus pressed the starter and the 4-cylinder turbo engine purred to life. He engaged the clutch, shifted into first, and drove away.

Longinus drove for fifteen minutes and then expertly parked his Audi A5 Cabriolet on Mariahilfer Strasse.  He locked the Audi and crossed the street with Lin to his apartment.  Once inside, Longinus locked the door and gave Lin the keys.  He showed her where the bathroom was, and the bedroom if she needed to sleep.

Longinus said, "Well, I'd better move.  I'll call you and let you know how I make out.  And you'd better keep your Beretta at the ready."

"I will, and Lon," said Lin, "thank you."

Longinus smiled back at Lin.

"I'll find James and bring him back to you."

Then Longinus walked out of the room.

# CHAPTER ELEVEN

# *HEALING MINDS CENTER*

Longinus drove on Reitschulgasse, and soon pulled his black Audi A5 Cabriolet into the side parking lot reserved for visitors to the Healing Minds Center.  He carefully parked between two Mercedes-Benz sedans, and then locked his car and set the alarm.  Longinus took a quick look at the outside of the building and saw that it consisted of four floors, and remembered that Ross was on the second floor in room 212.  He also made special note of the fire escapes.  Then he scanned both sides of the street.

*Nothing unusual,* he thought.

Longinus sauntered to the entrance and the double paned glass doors automatically hissed open.  The information desk was located just to the left, exactly how Lin had described it to him.  A young Chinese man greeted him.  It was the same attendant who had greeted Lin.

"May I help you, sir?" politely asked Yeung.

"Yes," said Longinus.  "My brother was brought in here last night. His name is James Ross."

"He's your brother?" asked Yeung.

"Yes.  I'd like to visit," said Longinus.

Yeung replied, "Yes sir.  May I see you identification please, sir?"

Longinus reached into his suit coat pocket and pulled out his wallet.  "Here's my drivers license."

Yeung looked at the license.

"Very well, sir," said Yeung handing him a clipboard.  "Here, please sign the visitors log."

Longinus picked up a pen and signed the visitors log on the clipboard.

Yeung smiled at Longinus.

"Thank you, Mister Inus," said Yeung as he handed Longinus back his drivers license.  "Take the elevator to the second floor.  Your brother is in room 212."

Longinus nodded and walked to the elevator.

*That was easy enough,* he thought to himself.

Longinus rode the elevator to the second floor and got out.  He walked slowly down the hall, noticing the various nurses and medical technicians roaming about.

*Looks pretty much like a normal clinic,* he thought.

He arrived at room 212 and peered through the window.  No one was in the room except for Ross lying in bed with an infusion running. Longinus knocked on the door and then entered.

"James, it's me, Lon," he said.

Ross turned to him with a blank stare on his face.

"Hello brother," said Ross mechanically, lacking affect.

*Brother?* thought Longinus. *Someone must have informed him that his brother was coming up to visit.*

There was already a chair pulled up beside the hospital bed waiting for a visitor.

Longinus sat down and said, "How are you doing, James?"

Ross replied, "I'm fine."

*Something's not right,* thought Longinus.

"What happened to you?" asked Longinus.

Ross replied, "I was drinking, and must have had too much and passed out. The next thing I remember was riding in an ambulance to the hospital."

Longinus looked puzzled.

"Why are you still here?" he asked.

Ross said, "The doctor told me I was dehydrated and needed fluids. That's why I have the IV."

Longinus stood up and walked over to where Ross's infusion was pumping. The plastic bag hanging had a sticker on it saying *Lactated Ringer's.*

*Okay that makes sense,* thought Longinus. *That's what someone gets when he's dehydrated.*

Longinus sat back down and said, "When can I take you home, James?"

"I can answer that," said a voice from the doorway.

Longinus turned around quickly.

It was Qiang.

"I'm Doctor Wu Qiang. I've been treating your brother."

Longinus stood up and walked over to the doctor.

"I'm pleased to meet you," said Longinus extending his hand. "I'm Lon Inus."

Wu shook hands and said, "Your brother gave us quite a scare. He was very dehydrated, so we needed to restore his electrolyte balance."

Longinus nodded.

"How's he doing now?"

Wu said, "He's much better now, and I can release him for home. He'll need some medicine, and I took the liberty to fill this prescription for you." Wu reached into his lab coat and pulled out a bottle of pills.

"Make sure he takes one every three hours until the whole bottle is finished," said Wu.

Longinus took the bottle and read off the label.

"Electrolyte tablets?" he asked.

Wu said, "Yes. He'll need to continue taking them for the next week. We don't want him to have a relapse."

Wu reached into his lab coat and pulled out his card.

"Here's how to contact me at this clinic if you need to," said Wu.

Mei Fang entered the room dressed in white as a nurse. "Sir, I'm here to remove the patient's IV."

Wu said, "Good, that'll take care of that, and all I need you to do, sir, is sign these discharge papers." Wu handed Longinus a discharge summary sheet and asked him to sign on the back. Longinus complied.

Wu said, "That covers it. Do you have any more questions, sir?"

Longinus said, "No. I'm ready to take him home."

Mei walked over to Ross and prepared her equipment on a chux pad at the bedside tray table. She closed off the tubing flow port and swabbed the area around the catheter site with a small alcohol pad.

Ross watched her.

Then she peeled back the tape, carefully removed the catheter, applied pressure with a small folded gauze pad, and wrapped Coban around it. She held pressure for a few seconds and stared back at Ross.

*Too bad,* she thought.

*It's just too bad he had to be the one.*

Then her and Doctor Qiang left the room and closed the door.

"Okay James, let's get you dressed," said Longinus.

Ross got out of bed and went to the room closet. Inside was hanging his freshly cleaned and pressed black suit and white cotton shirt. He dressed quickly, cinching his collar with the four-in-hand knot of his narrow black necktie. Ross found his wallet and cellphone also inside the closet and pocketed them. Then he looked at himself in the room mirror. He ran his hand through his hair to try and push it off his forehead, but it just fell back down again.

"Ready to go?" asked Longinus.

"I'm ready," said Ross. "Let's go."

Longinus walked to the door and opened it. Outside the room was Mei Fang waiting with a wheelchair.

"This is protocol, sir," explained Mei. "We don't want any of our patients tripping or falling down on the way out. Now, if you could just pull your car around to the front, I'll bring Mister Ross down to it."

Longinus nodded and hurriedly left to get his Audi.

Mei placed Ross in the wheelchair and escorted him to the front entrance of the clinic.

Mei felt sorry for Ross.

*His mind has been manipulated and was now susceptible to control from Doctor Qiang. They don't call him the Warlock for nothing,* she thought.

*And the pills given to Ross weren't electrolytes, but scopolamine. The longer he took them, the longer he would be controllable.*

Mei didn't know all the details of the plan, but she knew it was a big one. Only Doctor Wu knew exactly what the mission for Ross would be. But she did know that Ross would be activated for the mission by a codeword sent either by phone call or text message.

*How can they take a man and simply destroy his life like this?* she thought. *They not only brainwashed him, they have destroyed his very soul.*

Mei ran her fingers through the dark brown bangs of hair that fell across Ross's forehead. She tried to brush them up, but they just fell back down only in more disarray.

*This just isn't right,* she thought.

*Not to him.*

*Not to this man.*

Longinus arrived in his Audi and placed it in park with engine running, right in front of the spot where Ross and Mei Fang were waiting.

"Okay Mister Ross," said Mei, "here we go." And Mei walked Ross over to Longinus and the opened passenger door of the Audi.

Ross sat down and Mei closed the door.  Longinus placed the Audi in gear and drove slowly away from the Healing Minds Center.

Mei thought to herself, *I hate this job.*

# CHAPTER TWELVE

# MANCHURIAN CANDIDATE

Longinus was disturbed with the way Ross had responded to him at the Healing Minds Center.  While driving Ross back to the hotel, he decided to probe him a little.

"So, what really happened James?" asked Longinus.

Ross's expression didn't change.

"What do you mean, Lon?" replied Ross.

Longinus said, "Why did you pass out?  I mean, I left you both at the hotel lounge, dancing, and the next thing I know I'm being called in the morning that you collapsed from a suspected drugging?"

Ross's mind had been programmed for such a query.

"I drank a little too much," repeated Ross robotically.  "I'm sorry I worried you so much, brother."

Longinus cast a quick glance at Ross.

*What is he talking about?* thought Longinus.

*Is he joking with me?*

*Brother?*

*Yeah, I told the people at the clinic that I was his brother just to get in to see him as a relative. But does he think I am his real brother? This can't be right.*

Longinus probed him some more.

"What happened between you and Lin?"

Ross regurgitated the prepared response he was programmed to say by Doctor Wu Qiang, the Warlock.

"Who?" said Ross.

Longinus said, "Lin Sparrow, you know, who you were with at the lounge last night?"

Ross said, "I danced with so many, I just can't remember."

Longinus thought to himself, *What the hell? Does he have amnesia? What did they do to him at the clinic? It must have been a crash course in brainwashing.*

Then he glanced over at Ross again.

*They must have really worked the poor bastard over.*

Longinus deliberately drove slow through Innere Stadt and was coming up the long way on Herrengasse. They passed the government quarter and drove around the Hofburg Palace. Ross continued to stare mechanically straight ahead.

*He's not acknowledging the Hofburg,* thought Longinus. *He's not even looking at it. I'll try one more thing.*

Longinus was quickly coming up on the heart of the 1st District and all its various restaurants.

"It's been a long day James. Are you hungry?" asked Longinus.

"Yes," replied Ross.

Longinus flipped on his turn signal and pulled the Audi into the parking lot of his favorite French restaurant, Le Salzgries, on number six Marc Aurel Strasse.

"Let's get something to eat here," said Longinus as he parked the Audi.

"Okay," said Ross as he unbuckled his seatbelt.

Longinus studied Ross's mannerisms and was befuddled.

*Something's not right with the man,* he thought.

He watched Ross walk into the restaurant and knew something was wrong.

*The guy's walking with slouched shoulders,* he thought. *The James Ross I know always threw his shoulders back and walked proudly.*

Walking inside, Ross and Longinus were immediately greeted by headwaiter Günter.

"Guten abend meine Herren," said Günter. He immediately recognized Longinus as one of their regular customers. "Ah Mister Inus, so good to see you again, sir."

Günter looked to be in his early forties. He was wearing an older style dark blue Armani suit with inch-and-a-half lapels, and a Bellamy white laced Victorian shirt. His collar was open and he had it accented by a Gusleson dark burgundy floral ascot. Standing at six-foot-two and weighing two hundred pounds, Günter was stout and had the broken nose of a boxer. His head was completely shaved, and he sported a large drooping dark brown mustache.

"Fine, fine," answered Longinus.

"Two for dinner this evening, mein Herr?" asked Günter.

Longinus nodded. "Yes, two for dinner please."

Günter picked up two menus and led them to the smoking area, where Longinus always ate.

"Here you are sir," said Günter, pointing to a table. "I'll send your waitress right over." Günter raised his arm and snapped his fingers for the waitress. A blonde waitress scurried over to the table.

Nineteen-year-old Brigitte Arnné had been a waitress at Le Salzgries for the past eight months. Brigitte was a native of Innsbruck and working as a waitress to pay for her philosophy degree from the University of Vienna. Today she was wearing a red Shein Vcay dress with square neck and shirred waist ruffle hem. The dress was tight across her breasts and low in the back. It was cinched to her waist by a two-inch-wide black leather belt with silver baroque buckle. Her feet were nestled in three-inch-heeled black baroque shoes resplendent with matching silver baroque buckles. Her blonde hair was in twin French braids with tiny thin curls reaching to her eyebrows. Her beautiful face was reminiscent of a young Kim Basinger. Brigitte wore purple lipstick with a wet gloss to accent her sensuous mouth. Her fingernails were cut short and painted gloss highland green. She smelled of Florecita eau de parfum. Brigitte radiated a healthy, fun-loving, joyful ambience.

Ross looked at the menu.

"What do you recommend here, Lon?"

Longinus thought, *I just ate with James here a couple days ago. Has he totally forgotten?*

Longinus said, "Everything is good."

Brigitte said, "May I take your order please?"

Ross said quickly, "I'll have the cheeseburger classic with fries."

Brigitte started writing on her little pad.

"And to drink?" she asked.

Ross replied, "Coke."

Brigitte bit her lower lip and frowned.  "I'm sorry we don't have Coke, only Pepsi."

Ross said automatically, "Pepsi then."

Longinus furrowed his brow and knew something was wrong.

Brigitte looked at Longinus and asked, "And you sir?"

Longinus said, "I'll have the filet mignon, medium, with haricots verts and a salad."

Brigitte wrote it down on her little pad.

"What salad dressing would you like?" she asked.

"Um, Italian please," said Longinus, "and bring me a bowl of French onion soup."

"And to drink?"

"Bring me a tall Märzenbier," said Longinus.

Brigitte looked up from her notepad and smiled.  "I'll have that right out for you," she said.

Longinus gathered the menus and handed them to Brigitte.

She smiled and walked away, but the scent of her perfume lingered.

*This is not right,* thought Longinus. *Something is definitely wrong with James.  He made a big deal out of ordering French onion soup last time.  That's his favorite food.  He orders it anywhere and everywhere he goes. And he doesn't even ask for it now? No way. The poor guy has had something done to him, something sinister.  He's been hypnotized or brainwashed.*

Longinus reached inside his suit pocket and pulled out his Muratti Ambassador brand cigarettes. He tapped the packet with the crook of his left forefinger and extracted one.

*And James still thinks I'm his brother? No. Something is very wrong here.*

Longinus pulled out a black Ronson Comet lighter. He popped open the top and flicked the thumbwheel downward, igniting a wavering bluish flame. He eyed Ross as he was lighting his cigarette.

Ross was staring at the flame. He seemed mesmerized.

Longinus cocked his head to the side and allowed himself the luxury of a long, slow draw. The Centurian held the smoke in his lungs for a moment, and then tilted his head upwards hissing the tobacco vapors out through his nostrils.

*I'll try something,* he thought.

"What do you hear from sis?" asked Longinus.

Ross was under the mind control of Doctor Wu Qiang, the Warlock. He had gone through anticholinergic drugging, and transcranial direct current stimulation with propagandized hypnotic stimulation. He had a mission to complete, and had to obey the orders he was given.

"I've heard nothing," answered Ross.

*That cinches it,* thought Longinus. *The man is gone.*

Just then Brigitte returned with a tray load of food.

"Be careful gentlemen, the plates are very hot," gushed Brigitte.

"Thank you," said Longinus.

Ross had a distant look on his face.

Longinus prayed silently.

*God, allow me to help this young man.  Give him back his memory, Lord.  Deliver us from the evil one, and protect us in battle.  In the name of your most holy son Jesus, I ask this, amen.*

Longinus asked, "When do you have to go back to your unit, James?"

Ross's face took on a faraway look.

"Soon," he replied, "but I've got something to do here first."

"What would that be, James?" asked Longinus.

"Sorry Lon, it's classified," said Ross.

Longinus nodded.

Then the two soldiers turned their concentration to their lunch.

# CHAPTER THIRTEEN

# DIPLOMATIC SECURITY

The Diplomatic Security Service (DSS) is the security branch of the US Department of State. It conducts criminal investigations, threat analysis, cybersecurity, counterterrorism, counterintelligence, and personal protection of people, property, and information for the US State Department. Consisting of approximately 2500 special agents, the DSS is tasked with protecting visiting foreign dignitaries and US diplomatic missions abroad.

Today, a DSS team from the US Embassy in Vienna was dispatched to track down and recover the mythical World War Two Nazi time machine known as *the Bell* and codenamed *Die Glocke*. The team consisted of four special agents and one Special Assistant to the US Ambassador. They were Clive Maxsted, Erwin Foxwell, Charles Knight, Douglas Daniels, and Johnny Briggs. Foxwell and Knight were ex-military officers, Daniels and Briggs joined right out of college, and Maxsted was the Special Assistant to the US Ambassador.

They were having dinner at the Hofburgstüberl Cafe and discussing the mission they had been tasked to complete.

"Sir, do you really think this Bell or Die Glocke actually exists?" asked Knight.

Maxsted replied, "Something exists.  Whether it is the Bell or something else, it is up to us to find out and secure it."

Foxwell said, "If Captain Ross has it then he must be waiting for the right time to hand it over to State."

Maxsted looked at Foxwell cynically.

"Remember back in the Philippines when we first ran into Ross?" said Maxsted.

Foxwell searched his memory.

"You mean that's the same guy that's here now?" he asked.

Maxsted nodded his head affirmatively.

"Yes, this is him.  James Ross, Captain, US Army Special Forces. Back then he was on Jolo Island with that secret service agent purportedly to rescue a CIA man.  Ross is a loose cannon on deck.  He was out of control back then, and if he's involved in this then he's well out of his mission parameters."

Briggs said, "But if it is Ross, what is he doing here?  Why is he in Vienna?"

Maxsted became visibly irritated.

"It's Ross all right.  I checked."

"Yes sir," replied Briggs.

Maxsted was a career State Department official and had hated Ross since that Philippine episode.  He loathed the military and especially Special Forces.  He considered SF men to be overrated and egotistical.

"Ross stretches the rules and has no regard for authority. He thinks he is untouchable because of that green beret he wears. If Ross is holding back information about Die Glocke, I can assure you I'll find out," said Maxsted.

Daniels tried to change the subject.

"Sir, do we know where to look for the Bell?" he asked.

Maxsted said, "We have overhead IMINT that it's in a garden field outside the Hofburg Palace. But the field is completely covered with snow now. I mean, you can barely make out any of the statues."

Daniels nodded.

"And," said Maxsted, "we can't cause an international incident by roaming around the Hofburg gardens looking for a mythical time machine."

Maxsted clasped his hands together on the table and shook his head.

"No," Maxsted said, "we need to find and locate James Ross first, and then get him to lead us to Die Glocke."

Foxwell asked, "Are there any of the opposition around, sir?"

Maxsted replied, "Yeah. There's a Chinese team trying to locate the Bell, and supposedly a Mossad team as well."

The four DSS special agents looked at each other around the table.

Briggs rubbed his hands together.

"This could prove to be very interesting," said Briggs.

Maxsted leaned forward across the table.

"Listen," said Maxsted, "we are here to secure a vintage piece of World War Two German equipment. That's all. It's an antique. Of course the Chinese want it, and the Israelis."

Foxwell said, "There's a piece missing here, sir. I mean, we were all briefed that four Chinese nationals were shot to death inside the Hofburg chapel just a couple days ago. What were they doing in the chapel at midnight?"

Maxsted was about to burst.

"Agent Foxwell, that's classified information. As far as the Chinese nationals, they were the Chinese Archaeology Team sent to make a copy of the Spear of Destiny for their country. They were overcome by toxic fumes in the crypts below the chapel while on a tour. Apologies have already been made to President Xi Jinping by State. That's all we're prepared to say on the matter. We can't cause an international incident. Negotiations between our two countries is always fragile. China is expanding its empire and purchasing land and property everywhere. They've got the port in the Bahamas, the manufactured islands off the coast of Japan, farmland in our own country, factories in Mexico and Venezuela, Bagram Airfield in Afghanistan, and a weapons pact with Moscow. It is only a matter of time before they invade Taiwan."

Foxwell smiled, "I think President Trump will have something to say about that first, sir."

Maxsted leaned back in his chair and took a sip of his vodka and tonic.

"Don't get me started on that," said Maxsted. "Trump is visiting here tomorrow to meet with President Xi. Did you forget that?"

Foxwell looked nervously around the table at his other special agents.

"No sir. I didn't forget," he said.

"Our job at State is *diplomacy,* Special Agent Foxwell.  Diplomatic discussions and reasoning.   Not *gunboat-diplomacy* like Ross and Trump revel in.  And if I were you," said Maxsted, "I'd never make the mistake of bringing this subject up again."

"Yes sir," said Foxwell visibly embarrassed.

*He shouldn't talk to me like that,* thought Foxwell.  *He's got no right to embarrass me in front of the others.*

Then the waitress arrived with their dinners.

# CHAPTER FOURTEEN

# TRIGGER

Longinus knew he had to get Ross back to the hotel and in front of Lin.

*She's got to see him, talk to him,* he thought.

*However the Chinese have brainwashed him, whatever they've infected him with, he was infected first a long time ago by the love of Lin Sparrow,* he thought. *That love has to be strong enough to break this spell.*

Longinus and Ross finished their dinner.

"I've got to use the restroom," said Longinus. "Excuse me."

He pushed his chair back and slowly walked to the restroom. Once inside a stall, Longinus pulled out his cellphone and called Lin.

"Hello?" said Lin.

Whispering, Longinus said, "Lin, this is Lon. I'm with James. Everything went well at the clinic, and there was no trouble signing him out, but there's something definitely just not right."

"What do you mean?  What's wrong?" asked Lin.

Longinus tried to explain to her.  "I used the ruse of being his brother, a relative, to see him and sign him out.  But, he actually believes me to be his brother."

Lin said, "What else?"

"I took him to eat at my favorite French restaurant, Le Salzgries, on Marc Aurel Strasse."

"Okay," said Lin.

"And I watched James order a cheeseburger and fries.  This place has the best French onion soup in all of Vienna, and James Ross didn't order any, he ordered a cheeseburger and fries!  I watched him, just a couple days ago, order French onion soup here and make a big fancy deal out of it, and everyplace I've been with him he always asks if they have French onion soup, but not tonight."

Lin was shocked and just listened.

"So I thought I'd test him a little, and I asked him if he'd seen our sister, and he played along with me like we actually were brothers and had a sister!"

"My God," said Lin.  "He really is gone."

Longinus said, "But how, Lin?  How could the Chinese have brainwashed him so quickly?"

Lin thought for a second and pulled from her vast array of nursing knowledge.

"It is possible," she said.  "They had him for almost twenty-four hours.  It would have been a crash course in drugs, probably trans-cranial stimulation, and intense propaganda."

"Is there a way to quickly bring him back?" asked Longinus.

"Yes," said Lin. "The American CIA had a project called MK Ultra back in the 1950s. The Soviets stole it and taught it to the Chinese. It's the drugs that have the most lasting effect. Could be LSD, mescaline, scopolamine. Might be a combination of several."

Longinus felt he had to ask the next question.

"How long before it all wears off?" he asked.

Lin thought for a second.

"The worst is the medicine. Should be between 12-24 hours if he's separated from the drugs," she responded.

"What do you mean separated? He had an IV hanging on him at the clinic, but now there's nothing."

Lin said, "If he's being brainwashed for some kind of mission, then he could have a transdermal device under the skin on a time-release schedule."

Longinus said, "I don't see anything visible. Is there anyway I could check for something like that?"

"Yes," said Lin. "If they surgically implanted such a device it would most likely be on the forearm or the inner thigh."

*Oh great,* thought Longinus. *All I've got to do is get him to take off his coat and roll up his sleeves, or take off his pants.*

"What's the worst that could happen if they used the trans-cranial device?" asked Longinus.

Lin thought for a second.

"I'm not sure," she said. "But a combination of drugs and trans-cranial would make him or anyone extremely susceptible to propaganda, especially if all applied at once."

"What would the purpose be?" asked Longinus.

Lin said, "Considering his work, it could be some military objective, and most probably anti-American."

"How would they control him? I mean, how would they get him to do whatever it is they want?" asked Longinus.

Lin said, "There would be a sort of trigger mechanism."

"What?" said Longinus.

Lin said, "Yeah. There would be a trigger mechanism. It could be witnessing an event, perhaps listening to a certain song, or even hearing a certain word on a phone call, a codeword."

"Could this codeword be delivered in a text message?" asked Longinus.

"Yes," said Lin.

"So, if we know our Chinese friends as well as we think we do, basically James is a time bomb waiting to go off," said Longinus.

"Yes, it could be," said Lin. "If he really believes you're his brother, if he thinks he has a sister, and if he doesn't know about his obsession over French onion soup, then the Chinese have definitely done something heinous to him."

"Could it be that he was hypnotized?" asked Longinus.

Lin said, "Doubtful. Because you have to basically have the desire to be hypnotized. You have to want it. And his will is much stronger than that. But hypnotism can be tricky."

Longinus said, "How so?"

"Hypnotism can be used in conjunction with pharmaceuticals to bring about the desired effect," said Lin. "I think you should just get him back to the hotel."

Longinus looked around to make sure no one was watching him.

"I agree," he said. "I need to get him back to the Herrenhof Steigenberger. Meet us at his room. Once I get him to the hotel, how do you want to play it?"

Lin said, "I need to see him. I believe you, and I know something was done to James. I'll be able to check him for any surgical implant."

"Lin," said Longinus, "when I mentioned you, he acted as if he didn't know you."

Lin started to tear up.

"It's okay," she said. "Bring him back to the room and both of us will take it one step at a time."

"Right," said Longinus. "We'll be there soon." Then he hung up the phone.

Longinus stood up and flushed Ross's pills down the toilet. Then he walked out of the men's room and back to the table.

"Ready to go, James?" asked Longinus.

"Sure Lon," replied Ross.

Longinus thought, *He still seems blank, like he's sleep walking.*

Longinus glanced at the check and left seventy-five euros.

"Let's go," said Longinus.

Ross stood up automatically and followed Longinus to the door.

"Come back soon gentlemen," said Brigitte, waving to the pair as they walked out the door.

Longinus glanced skyward. Glistening snowflakes where softly floating down in the dark, illuminated by a full moon and the iridescent lamp posts high overhead.

"Such a beautiful December night," he said.

Ross just continued walking towards the car.

Then Longinus hunched up his shoulders against the cold and followed Ross towards the Audi.

Once inside, Longinus pressed the starter, engaged the clutch, and put the Audi in gear. The engine purred gently in the stillness of the night.

He carefully steered out of the parking lot and onto the street.

"I'll bet you'll be glad to get back to your room, James," said Longinus.

Ross stared straight ahead.

"Don't you think so, James? Don't you think you'll be happy to get back to the hotel?" asked Longinus again.

"Yes Lon, I will," said Ross.

"How much longer are you on leave, James? You know, from your unit?" asked Longinus.

Ross said, "I'm not on leave, brother."

Longinus looked puzzled. He said, "But I thought you were on military leave?"

Ross stared unblinkingly ahead.

"I'm on a mission," said Ross.

Longinus said, "What?"

Ross repeated. "I'm on a mission, brother."

"What do you mean?" asked Longinus.

Ross said, "I'm on the most important mission of my life."

"What?" said Longinus. "What is it?"

Ross turned his head mechanically and looked at Longinus.

"You know I can't tell you, brother. But when it is done, you will be very proud of me."

Longinus said, "I'm proud of you now.  You never mentioned a mission before."

Ross said, "It will all be over in two days' time, and then the whole world will be a much safer place."

For the first time, Longinus was really scared.

# PART THREE

*I laugh at those who think they can damage me.  They do not know who I am, they do not know what I think, they cannot even touch the things which are really mine and with which I live.*

Epictetus
50 — 135 AD
Greek Stoic Philosopher

# CHAPTER FIFTEEN

# STRANGER

Longinus drove deliberately slow.  Large flakes of wet snow were plummeting down more plentiful as the black Audi A5 Cabriolet made its way towards the hotel.  Inus flicked on the windshield wipers, allowing Ross to take in the sights.  The evening  was vibrantly alive with red and green twinkling Christmas lights everywhere.  Long silver strands of tinsel were strung across lamp posts giving them a chandelier-type appearance.  Frosted merchant shop windows displayed everything from electronic toys to the latest designer fashions.  An ocean of taxis were beeping their horns and zooming in and out of storefront parking.  Couples were engulfed by the sights and sounds of the Viennese holiday season.  Their breath was coming out in puffs as one, circling and disappearing skyward as they huddled closer, arm-in-arm, with smiles on their faces.  It was the hustle and bustle of the merriest time of year in Austria.  It was a scene reminiscent of a Charles Dickens novel.

*Maybe this will bring back some memories for James,* thought Longinus. *At any rate it can't hurt.*

Soon they were at the Herrenhof Steigenberger Hotel. Longinus pulled the Audi in front of the valet parking station. Ross and Longinus got out, and the young valet exchanged a blue ticket for the keys.

"I'll take care of it, sir," said the valet to Longinus.

Ross and Longinus walked to the entrance of the Herrenhof Steigenberger Hotel. The heavy glass entrance doors automatically hissed open for them. They walked to the front desk.

"Room 323 please," said Longinus.

Ross stood staring straight ahead.

The receptionist gave Longinus the key and he and Ross headed for the elevators.

They walked past the small convenience shop next to the restaurant, and Longinus noticed a copy of the Heute, Vienna's top newspaper, with headlines proclaiming *Trump and Xi Summit Tomorrow.*

Longinus thought, *Trump and Xi are having a summit here tomorrow? And James says the most important mission of his life takes place tomorrow? My God. Could he be programmed to disrupt the summit? Or perhaps worse? Much worse? My God.*

They rode the elevator to the third floor, only this time Ross was staring at Longinus.

The elevator stopped and the doors slowly opened.

Ross said, "Give me the key Lon, I can take it from here."

Longinus could do nothing but hand over the key to his friend.

*I didn't get a chance to check his arms for an implant,* thought Longinus. He watched Ross mechanically turn and walk towards his room. Longinus spotted a comfort chair next to the bank of elevators and sat down.

*I think I'd better just hang around and wait.*

Ross inserted the plastic credit-card-type door key into the slot until the light turned green. Then he opened the door and stepped inside. Hearing someone enter, Lin Sparrow immediately walked out of the bedroom.

"James!" she exclaimed.

Lin ran over to Ross and threw her arms around him.

"Oh my darling," she said, "I'm so sorry. I tried to see you in the hospital, but they wouldn't let me. Are you all right now? How do you feel?"

Lin reached up and kissed Ross on the lips.

Ross looked at Lin as if she was a stranger.

Lin gazed deeply into Ross's eyes, but the eyes staring back didn't register a flicker of remembrance for her.

She hugged him again, and this time placed her head on his chest.

"Oh Jamie, I was so worried about you, so scared," Lin said.

But James Ross had no recollection.

"Excuse me, but what are you doing in my room?" said Ross.

Lin stiffened and stood back as if hit with a bucket of ice water.

"My God, what have they done to you?" asked Lin desperately.

But Ross kept looking through her, past her.

"What do you mean?" he said robotically.

Lin reached up and lovingly took his face in her hands.

"What's the matter with you?" she pleaded.

"Don't you know me?  Don't you know me?"

Ross grabbed her wrists and pulled her hands from his face.

"You are mistaken," he said disdainfully.

"I've never seen you before in my life."

# CHAPTER SIXTEEN

# PARADOX

Inside room 323, Ross took off his black suit coat and threw it on a chair. He started to unbutton his shirt sleeves.

"Look, you're going to have to leave now, because all I want to do is take a hot shower," said Ross as he removed his shirt.

Lin saw the small bandage on his right forearm and pointed to it.

"What is that?" she asked.

Ross looked at his forearm and became confused.

"I — I don't know," he said.

In a flash, Lin grabbed his arm and ripped off the bandage. She felt the lump under his skin.

Lin screamed, "This is an implant! Someone has surgically implanted something under your skin!"

Sitting in a chair by the bank of elevators on the third floor, Longinus looked at his 1940 Eterna chronograph wristwatch.

*God I wish something would happen,* he thought.

Then he heard Lin's scream.

Longinus sprang up and ran to their door and pounded on it.

"Lin!  Let me in!  This is Lon!" he yelled.

Lin Sparrow ducked under Ross's arm and hurried to the door.

Then Ross's Samsung Galaxy Stratosphere II cellphone buzzed.

"Hello?" answered Ross.

Lin unlocked the door and let Longinus in, then relocked it.

Ross accidentally had the phone on speaker.

"Paradox," said a voice on the phone.

Ross visibly stiffened.

Lin and Longinus stopped dead in their tracks and stared at Ross.

"Paradox," said the voice on the phone again.

Longinus said, "What's going on?"

Lin answered quickly, "He's got a surgical implant on his right forearm, and now I think he's being activated."

"Paradox," said the voice on the cellphone once more.

Ross's eyes glazed over as he mechanically responded to the voice on the phone.  He said, "Ready to comply."

The voice was Doctor Wu Qiang, the Warlock.  He had just issued Ross the trigger codeword to set the operation into motion.

Wu said, "Tomorrow at six o'clock in the evening you will go to the Hofburg Congress Center.  You will wait outside until United States President Donald Trump and Chinese President Xi Jinping are departing.  Then you will kill them both."

Longinus couldn't believe his ears.

Lin started to move towards Ross, but Longinus held her back.

"Wait," he whispered to her.

The Warlock's voice on the phone said, "After you kill them both you will kill yourself.  Understand?"

Ross mechanically said, "Yes."

Then the phone went dead.

Longinus lunged forward with his QSW Chinese pistol and smashed it across the back of Ross's skull.  Ross collapsed to the floor in a heap.  Then Longinus immediately took a knee beside him and in a flash flicked out his Italian Rizzuto stiletto.  In one quick slash he cut the scopolamine capsule out of Ross's forearm.

"Sorry James," said Longinus.

Lin, overcoming her immediate state of shock, said, "Come on, help me get him into bed."

They carried Ross and laid him on the bed.  Lin stripped off his clothes and pulled the blanket up to his waist.  She went to the bathroom and came back with a cold washcloth to place on his forehead, and one to stop the bleeding from his arm.

"How long will he be out?" asked Lin.

Longinus said, "Maybe thirty minutes.  I'm sorry I had to do that, Lin."

Lin shook her head.  "There was no other way," she said.  "I'm just thankful you did it so quickly."

Lin looked at Longinus and said, "So what happens now?"

Longinus sat down in a bedroom chair.  He said, "Tell me, how long before whatever it was they did to him wears off?"

Lin said, "Hang on."

She walked out of the bedroom and picked up off the floor the tiny capsule that Longinus had cut out of Ross's arm.

Then she went to the bathroom and flushed the capsule down the toilet.

Lin walked back into the bedroom and saw that Longinus had tied Ross's hands and feet together with his and Ross's belts.

"I'm willing to bet they used an anticholinergic drug on James," said Lin. "Probably one like scopolamine. If they did, then it has a half-life of nine hours. So that would be tomorrow morning. But there's an antidote to these drugs which can reverse it pretty quick. It's called physostigmine."

"Hey," said Longinus, "there's an all-night pharmacy right down the street. The owner is a friend of mine. He's been treating me for years. Do you have a pen and piece of paper?"

Lin opened the bedside desk drawer and gave Longinus a piece of hotel letterhead stationary and a pen. Longinus wrote a note to his friend and then gave the letter to Lin.

"The name of the pharmacy is Holy Spirit. Ask for Howard. Show him this note and tell him it's for me. Just write down here what you want and he'll give it to you," said Longinus. "You'd better bundle up though. It's cold out there."

"Oh my God Lon, I don't know how to thank you enough," said Lin.

Longinus said, "My thanks will be seeing James recover."

Lin hurriedly picked up Ross's clothes from the floor where she had thrown them and hung them up in the closet. Then she put on her red wool jacket and google-mapped the location of Holy Spirit Pharmacy.

"I'll be back as quick as I can," said Lin.

"We'll be here," said Longinus managing a smile.

Lin took Ross's velcro wallet as a precaution. Once down in the lobby, she inputed the name of the pharmacy into her iPhone global positioning system (GPS).

*It's just around the corner here,* she thought to herself.

Lin walked out of the front double doors of the Steigenberger. It was already dark, and a gust of frigid December air hit her. She turned up her collar and thrust her hands into her pockets. Outside in front of the hotel was an elegant complimentary horse-drawn carriage.

*Looks like Cinderella,* she thought.

The driver of the carriage leaned over and said to Lin, "Give you a ride, Missy?"

*Missy?* thought Lin. *That's a little strange for Vienna.*

Lin waved him off.

"Not tonight, no thank you," she said.

Out of her peripheral vision Lin saw two men suddenly emerge from the dark shadows. They were dressed in black overcoats and looked like secret police. One grabbed her by the arm and the other flashed a badge.

"I'm Special Agent Erwin Foxwell, ma'am, of the United States Diplomatic Security Service," he said. "We'd like you to come with us and answer some questions."

Lin struggled against agent Charles Knight, who had her by the arm.

"Not now," Lin protested. "I'm on my way to the pharmacy."

Agent Douglas Daniels was the driver in the carriage. Sitting behind him was agent Johnny Briggs.

"Please step into the carriage, ma'am," Daniels said.

"Yes ma'am, please don't make a scene," said Knight.

"I'll do worse that that," said Lin.

"HELP! RAPE! HILFE! VERGEWALTIGEN!" screamed Lin at the top of her lungs.

Then she reached up with both hands and took a hold of Knight's coat and pulled him close to her and kicked him hard in his crotch.

"Umph!" said Knight, doubling over on the snowy sidewalk.

Lin took off running towards the pharmacy as strolling couples outside stopped and stared, and started gathering about to see what all the commotion was.

Special Agent Daniels leaned forward and said, "Pick him up and get in the carriage. We'll follow her."

Foxwell helped Knight into the carriage and Daniels tapped the horse's behind with his whip.

"Let's go horse," said Daniels.

The horse clip-clopped, clip-clopped, down the dark snowy street following after Lin Sparrow.

Lin ran as fast as she could, trying not to slip on the snow-covered pavement, and dodging around to avoid the strolling couples. Her breath was coming out in huge puffs as her throat and lungs began to burn from the sudden intake of frigid wintry air. She saw a large brightly lit yellow neon sign up ahead for the Holy Spirit Pharmacy and she ducked inside.

"There she goes," said Special Agent Briggs pointing with his finger. "She went into that pharmacy there."

Foxwell said, "Pull up in front."

The carriage was just about in front of the pharmacy when a black Mercedes-Benz sedan quickly cut in front and blocked them.

"What the hell is this?" yelled Daniels.

The headlights of the Mercedes-Benz temporarily blinded the horse and she turned her head away. The back two doors of the Mercedes opened and two men dressed in dark suits approached the carriage.

"Sorry," said Yitzhak Zanir. "Hope we didn't startle your horse."

Yitzhak Zanir was the Kidon commissioned leader of the Mossad team.

The two Mossad agents leaned into the carriage and brandished suppressed Masada 9mm pistols.

DSS Special Agent Erwin Foxwell held up his hand. "Now wait just one minute here. We are United States Diplomatic Security. We have jurisdiction here. You are interfering with a sensitive matter of United States foreign policy."

Zanir frowned and said, "My dear special agent, the woman you so rudely tried to detain is a friend of ours."

"A personal friend," chimed in Benjamin Shiloah.

Zanir said, "Yes that's right. And we had plans to have dinner with her tonight. So you see, it would be better for everyone if you just drove away and left us all in peace."

Foxwell pulled out his badge and credentials and held them in front of Zanir's face.

"I'm ordering you all to stand down," said Foxwell.

Shiloah looked at Zanir and said, "He's ordering us."

Foxwell was visibly irritated.

"Now!" demanded Foxwell.

Zanir smiled and said, "He said 'now.' He wants us to stand down now."

Then Shiloah took a hold of the horse's bridle and started to walk her back into the street. The DSS men decided the better part of valor would be to just retreat. The horse clip-clopped, clip-clopped, pulling the carriage full of DSS agents towards the 1st District and its elegant holiday illuminated nightlife.

Inside the pharmacy, Lin said, "Is Howard here?"

The sole person behind the counter looked over his reading glasses at Lin. "I'm Howard," he said.

Howard Blackham was a sixty-five-year-old Swiss pharmacist who had made Vienna his home over thirty years ago. Howard was balding with tuffs of gray hair surrounding his ears. In his early twenties, Howard had spent four years as a Kommando Spezialkräfte in the Swiss army and had damaged his knees from too many hundred-pound-full-equipment military parachute jumps in the Alps. He developed reactive arthritis and decided to use his disability pay to go to pharmacy college. He developed a lifelong friendship with Lon G. Inus over twenty-five years ago when Inus stopped an attempted robbery at the pharmacy and saved his life.

Lin gave Howard the note, and he saw that it was from Inus. He looked at Lin and smiled.

"You need physostigmine to treat anticholinergic overdose?" asked Howard. "Okay, I'll be right back."

Howard busied himself behind the counter and started filling several syringes.

Lin looked outside the window and saw the confrontation occur between Mossad and DSS.

"Howard, is it possible for me to use a back exit out of here?" asked Lin.

Howard had just finished preparing the medicine and placed it into a bag. He studied Lin for a second.

"Yes of course, mademoiselle. Come this way."

Lin asked, "How much do I owe you?"

"For Lon Inus — you owe me nothing," said Howard.

Howard gave Lin the bag of medicine and motioned for her to follow him. He led her into the storage room and unlocked the rear exit door for her.

"Tell Lon I said it's time for he and I to have lunch again," said Howard, holding the door open for her.

Lin said, "Thank you sincerely Howard." Then she walked through the doorway and disappeared into the blackness of the night.

The Mossad men were waiting out front to intercept Lin as she exited the pharmacy.

"What's taking her so long?" said Zanir.

Yatom peered into the pharmacy's steam covered front window and rubbed his hand across it.

"I don't see her," said Yatom.

"What?" asked Zanir.

"Maybe she's in the restroom," said Harel.

Zanir walked over and quickly looked in the window and then entered the pharmacy. Howard was diligently working behind the counter preparing prescriptions.

"Excuse me sir," Zanir said to Howard, "but wasn't there just a young lady in here?"

Howard looked carefully at Zanir over his reading glasses.

"Yes.  Yes there was," said Howard.

Zanir said, "Where is she?"

Howard said very carefully, "She's ah, gone."

Zanir shook his head and shrugged his shoulders.  Then he turned around and walked outside.

# CHAPTER SEVENTEEN

# MASTER PLAN

Doctor Wu Qiang had activated Ross with the trigger word *Paradox*. Ross was given the mission to assassinate the President of the United States and the President of the People's Republic of China at their Vienna summit meeting. The Warlock was out to inaugurate a war. If he only killed one, then the survivor would be blamed and war would start. If Ross was good enough to kill both, America would still be blamed and world war would start. If Ross couldn't manage to kill any of them, the United States would still be blamed because Ross would be viewed as an American assassin. The entire planet was ripe for a complete makeover. But Wu was not acting alone. He had a benefactor who had been sewing the seeds of discontent and hatred since 1945. His name was Ansgar Ludwig Nachtnebel.

Ansgar Ludwig Nachtnebel was currently ninety-one years old. He had grown up in Prussia, and witnessed the horrors of the economic depression that followed Germany's tragic loss in war.

In 1944 at the tender age of eleven, young Nachtnebel became a member of the Hitler Youth in Berlin. He grew quite a reputation for himself by turning in the locations of suspected Jews to the Nazi Schutzstaffel, or SS. In early 1945, Nachtnebel joined the 3rd SS Panzer Division Totenkopf, and fought savagely during the defense of Berlin. He was awarded the Nazi Iron Cross for bravery on the same day it was announced that the Führer had been killed in the fighting. Nachtnebel was taken prisoner by General Patton's Third Army in May 1945, and served four months in an allied prisoner of war camp in Wickrathberg. Upon his release, he was repatriated to England in 1946, where he first found employment as a bank clerk, and later moved up to bank teller. By the age of twenty-five, he had become a stockbroker and was soon on his way up the financial ladder. When he turned forty-five, he established his own European monetary fund, and had assets valued at over one billion dollars. Nachtnebel was a master at accumulating and then manipulating a country's currency by *selling short*. Selling short means an investor borrows stock shares that he believes will drop in price, then he sells those borrowed shares at market price, then he buys back the shares when the price drops. Finally, he returns the shares to the original lender, profiting from the difference. He amassed millions in Thai baht and the Malaysian ringgit, and later sold them short and thus tripled his investments. Nachtnebel was accused of deliberately crashing the economies of several countries for his personal profit. But his answer was that when the currencies start to decline, he purchases them to realize profits later based on his speculation. Triggering monetary crisis for fun and profit became his mantra. As an atheist, Nachtnebel was only concerned with making more and more money. He was not concerned with how his tactics affected the lives of ordinary people. Today, he is the Director General of the Nachtnebel New World Institute, which speculates in radical Marxist-Leninist approaches to reorganizing worldwide international financial systems.

Ansgar Nachtnebel and Doctor Wu Qiang met seven years ago at the World Psychotherapy Forum in Geneva, Switzerland. Nachtnebel was lecturing on his "Quantum Millionaire" theory that basically anyone, regardless of background, can become wealthy by selling short and betting on the future price of a stock. In Doctor Wu Qiang, he found a kindred heart that believed mankind was in need of a reboot. Doctor Qiang found his financial backer. Together they devised a plan, fictitiously at first, that would bring the world superpowers to the brink of war. Someone who could speculate on such an event would be able to make billions of dollars. After several meetings in Geneva, they decided that what was needed was to get the United States and China's economies to outspend each other through war. Everything came together in Vienna with the Trump/Xi summit. The Chinese teams were already in country with the Spear of Destiny mission, and all that was needed was the capture of an American soldier to be used as the patsy.

Doctor Wu Qiang knew certain death awaited him in China if it should ever be revealed that he had a hand in this conspiracy. But, like his friend Ansgar, Wu was willing to take the gamble. He was willing to risk his life for capitalist gains. He was speculating.

As far as Ansgar Nachtnebel was concerned — he was old, he wanted more billions for his children, and he was safe in his secure fortress compound in Zermatt Switzerland. Nachtnebel firmly believed the world was due for a complete reboot. He was ready to make it happen.


Lin Sparrow trudged through the snow and made it back to the Herrenhof Steigenberger Hotel. She rode the elevator to the third floor and walked down the plush red carpeted hall to room 323. Lin let herself in with the room key.

"Lon?" said Lin. "I've got the antidote."

"We're in the bedroom," said Longinus. "Come on in."

Ross was still unconscious and lying on the bed in the same position. His hands and feet were tied with belts, and his mouth was gagged with a handkerchief.

"How's he doing?" asked Lin.

"Okay. He's been out since you left," said Longinus. "But he's starting to stir. I had to gag him."

Lin pulled three syringes out of the paper pharmacy bag.

Longinus said, "Better give it to him quick before he fully wakes up."

Lin sat down next to Ross on the bed and wiped his right shoulder muscle with an alcohol pad. Then she administered the shot intra-muscularly into his deltoid.

Longinus asked, "How long before in takes effect?"

"Should be around three to eight minutes," she said. "Your friend Howard gave me enough to last all night if need be."

Lin held Ross by his hand and checked his pulse.

Ross was starting to stir slightly.

Longinus leaned over and removed the handkerchief gag from Ross.

"Do you think he was hypnotized too?" asked Longinus.

Lin said, "Doubtful.  Medical science has found that the subject has to want to be hypnotized for it to be effective.  And James has a strong mind.  He would have resisted with everything he had inside."

Longinus nodded.

Lin looked at her Citizen ProMaster Dive watch.

"We should know in a couple seconds," she said.

Ross slowly turned his head from side to side.  Then his eyelids began to flutter.

"Ahhhh," moaned Ross.

Then his eyes completely opened, and he glanced from Longinus to Lin.

"What the hell happened?" said Ross. "My head feels like somebody jammed it full of silly putty."

Lin smiled and leaned in and kissed Ross on his cheek, while Longinus proceeded to untie his hands and feet.

"Welcome back my friend," said Longinus.

Ross groaned as he pushed himself up in bed.

Lin asked, "What do you remember, Jamie?"

Ross said, "I remember feeling dizzy in the hotel lounge, and then the next thing I knew I woke up in some kinda hospital with a bunch of Chinese hovering around me."

"What else?" asked Longinus.

Ross said, "There were four of them, three men and one woman. The main guy was a doctor.  His name was Quack, or Qwok ..."

"No, wait a second. His name was Qiang — Doctor Wu Qiang," said Ross. "He told me they were going to turn me into a zombie. They were giving me stuff intravenously, and had headphones pounding me with propaganda, and some weird electrodes on my head."

Lin asked, "Do you remember the doctor mentioning what exactly was infusing into you?"

Ross searched his memory. "Yeah. It was something called scopolamine, I think. He said it would allow him to control me. They were going to turn me against the United States. They had some mission planned for me."

Lin picked up his hand and kissed it.

"I'm so glad you're back my love," said Lin.

She looked at Longinus and said, "What do you think, Lon?"

Longinus scratched his head and said, "Boy, that sure was crazy there for a while. Sorry I had to whack you on the head, James."

Ross felt the back of his head and said, "It's okay Lon."

Longinus looked at them both and said, "Please, someone tell me what is silly putty?"


It proved to be a long night, with Lin giving Ross two more injections just to be safe. She slept in the bed with Ross and snuggled to him. Longinus slept on the couch in the living room.

Ross awoke with the jolt of an electric spark. It was ten minutes before six o'clock in the morning. As usual, he had mentally impelled himself to wake up through sheer force of his will, a practice he had developed while attending the Special Forces Qualification Course.

So as not to wake Lin, he silently staggered into the bathroom, flicking on the lights. He turned on the shower and stepped in, not wasting any time. In three minutes his shower was over. Ross stepped out of the shower stall and wrapped one of the huge blue terrycloth hotel towels around his waist.

Wiping his right hand across the steam covered mirror, he looked at himself. He fingered his chin and reached for his AAFES shave gel. With a liberal amount of Army-Air-Force-Exchange-Services shave gel on, he slowly glided his razor across his face. He lowered his head towards the sink and splashed hot water across his face to rinse off the remaining residue. Finally, he poured Aqua Velva Ice Blue aftershave into his cupped left hand and slapped it on his face.

*Now that is refreshing,* he thought.

Ross tiptoed into the living room and saw Longinus still asleep on the couch. He went to the closet and quietly took out his clothes.

Returning to the bedroom, Ross dressed quickly. He stepped into a pair of green plaid boxer shorts, and then slipped into a white cotton shirt. He put on his black suit pants, black socks, and black leather shoes. He looked at himself in the bedroom mirror and tied a four-in-hand knot with his narrow black necktie, cinching it up to his collar. Ross ran a comb through his hair, and tried to push it up off his forehead, but it just fell back down again.

Ross crept back into the living room to the breakfast nook. As quietly as he could, Ross made a full pot of black coffee.

Longinus started to stir on the couch.

"Umph," said Longinus as he stretched his arms. "Good morning," he said. "How are you feeling today, James?"

Ross said, "I feel good, Lon."

Ross poured Longinus a cup of coffee and handed it to him.

"I want to thank you, you and Lin, for saving my life," said Ross.

Longinus nodded and said, "I'm just glad you're feeling better."

"Me too," said Lin, walking out of the bedroom wearing a large white hotel robe cinched at her waist.

Ross picked up another coffee mug and poured Lin a cup. He added one creamer and two Sweet & Lows. Lin took the coffee and sat down on the chair by the desk.

Ross took a seat and said, "The Chinese grabbed me and wanted to use me for a mission. Lin, in your estimation, how long do you think the drugs they gave me would have controlled me?"

Lin thought for a second. "Probably twenty-four to forty-eight hours," she said. "They had a tiny capsule of scopolamine surgically implanted under your skin."

Ross looked at the site on his right forearm.

"That capsule was time-releasing the drug into your body," said Lin.

"So," said Ross, "we can assume whatever they were planning was going to happen in a day or two."

Longinus said, "We heard what they were planning. You had the phone on speaker. These people wanted you to kill the presidents of both China and the United States."

Ross sat back and took a sip of his coffee.

Longinus snapped his fingers and said, "Listen, I saw a newspaper in the lobby saying that the Trump/Xi Jinping summit is happening this very evening at the Austrian Parliament Conference Center."

Ross took another sip of his coffee.

"That's it then," said Ross.

Lin said, "The puzzle starts to fit together."

Ross said, "They wanted to use me as a patsy. To have an American soldier do their killing."

"But why kill both presidents?" asked Longinus. "Why both?"

Lin looked at them and said prophetically, "Because someone else is pulling the strings. Someone who has another agenda."

Ross said, "Exactly. A fanatic like Doctor Wu Qiang would have to know that he would be executed if anything went wrong. He would say that he was just following his orders. He would say he gave the order, but something went wrong. And he would also have to know that if I had succeeded in killing both men, that he would surely be executed in China, mistake or not. So, his final orders to me had to come from a third party. Someone with a lot of money who wants to change the current world order."

"What do you mean?" asked Lin.

Ross said, "Doctor Qiang may have been given the order from the Ministry of State Security to develop an American soldier assassin. But there's no way he was tasked with the mission to assassinate their own leader, Xi Jinping. No. Qiang, for whatever reasons, may have figured his days working at MSS were numbered. He probably is on someone else's bankroll. Someone big enough to have plausible deniability."

Longinus said, "Someone with millions."

"Maybe billions," said Lin.

Ross stood up and started pacing back and forth.

"Well, thanks to you guys, we have destroyed their plans.  But I want this guy Qiang.  I want Doctor Wu Qiang," said Ross.

Longinus said, "James, it would be like walking into a hornets nest.  They would be waiting, perhaps in force with more assets.  I know you're upset — "

"Upset really isn't the word," interrupted Ross.

"I know, I know.  But you're back now.  The summit is tonight.  Doctor Qiang thinks you are still under his control.  That is an advantage for us," said Longinus.

Ross said, "You're right Lon.  We need to alert the president's detail, the secret service.  There may be more than one guy brainwashed at that summit.  The Chinese may have programed another patsy."

Lin spoke up, "Wait, there's more."

Longinus and Ross looked at her.

"What do you mean 'more' Lin?" asked Longinus.

Ross said, "Yeah.  What else?"

Lin explained, "When I went to the pharmacy, some men in a tourist carriage approached me."

Ross asked, "A tourist carriage?"

"Yes," said Lin.  "They were driving it.  They said they were from the United States Diplomatic Security Service, and that they wanted to ask me some questions."

Longinus looked at Ross.

Ross asked, "Do you remember their names?"

Lin said, "The one who showed me his badge was named Foxwell.  He said he was a special agent."

"What else?" asked Ross.

Lin said, "I sort of kicked one of them in his privates."

Ross looked at Longinus and both men smiled.

"Then what?" asked Longinus.

Lin said, "Inside the pharmacy I looked out the window and saw the same men who were in Zurich last week. Only now, they were having a confrontation with the diplomatic security guys. I recognized one of the men. His name is Yitzhak Zanir. He's Israeli. He works for Mossad."

Ross thought for a second. "Those guys can only be here because of Die Glocke. They want it. They tried last week, and now they've tracked you here and are trying to get it."

Lin said, "Why would Israel want Die Glocke?"

Longinus spoke up. "I think I can answer that. They would want it simply to keep it out of others hands, more nefarious hands. Israel would probably dismantle it. Don't you think so, James?"

Ross said, "Could be. Israel is fighting for their very survival. But the Diplomatic Security Service men — they've got to be here for the purpose to secure Die Glocke for the United States government. Our State Department wants to ship it back to the mainland, probably for research."

"Would they use it against an enemy?" asked Longinus. "Would they travel in time with it?"

Ross thought for a second. "I guess I wouldn't put it past certain elements in our State Department or Defense Department to do just that. Using Die Glocke to change the course of past historical events or future events is dangerous. You can disrupt certain elements. You can alter future outcomes.  You think you're doing good, but it can turn into a Frankenstein monster."

Lin said, "At one point you told me we need to destroy Die Glocke.  What do you think now, James?"

"Yeah," said Ross.  "More than ever we can't let any of them get a hold of that machine.  It's got to be destroyed."

# CHAPTER EIGHTEEN

# *GOOD GUYS WEAR BLACK*

Lin came out of the bedroom dressed in bluejeans, sneakers, a blue sweater, and red wool jacket. Ross was wearing his black suit with black sweater underneath, white cotton shirt, narrow black necktie, and black shoes. Longinus was in his black suit with long black overcoat.

Longinus said, "Better dress warm. It's cold out there."

"Lin, are you sure that jacket is enough for you?" asked Ross.

"Yes," said Lin. "I'll be fine."

Ross reached into the closet and took out his long black overcoat and handed it to her.

"Here, I'd feel better if you put this on," he said.

Then they all sat down to go over their plan one final time.

Ross said, "We've got three elements looking for Die Glocke: The Chinese team, the Mossad team, and the DSS team. They all want it for their respective countries. But, as we've all said, we can't let any country get this machine."

"Agreed," said Lin. "It's just too tempting and too dangerous in the wrong hands."

Longinus said, "I'm not well versed in these matters. But if you feel this is the right way to go, then we must."

Ross nodded. "We have to destroy it," he said. "There's probably imagery of Die Glocke resting in the field where Lin left it. But, to our advantage, Lin knows exactly where it is, and they don't, especially since it's totally covered with snow now. And I don't believe the Austrian government would take kindly to three teams of foreign agents rummaging about in the snow looking for it."

Longinus said, "And Lin has in her possession the only means to operate it, which is the dagger she carries. The foreign teams would have to manually forklift it out, because they wouldn't know why it can't be operated. At least I don't think they would."

Ross said, "I believe we can agree on that. So, first we need to alert the president's secret service detail of a pending threat, and then we need to get Die Glocke out of here."

Longinus said, "And the only way to do that is for you and Lin to fly it out, or whatever one actually does in a time machine."

Ross had been secretly wondering if Longinus wouldn't like to take a trip back in time, to undue the Spear of Destiny incident. But then he realized that if it was undone, the entire fabric of time would be altered, including the attempt to steal the spear which happened just last week.

Longinus looked at Lin and Ross with his sad, dark brown eyes.

"You and Lin need to get that machine out of here," said Longinus. "Take it somewhere and destroy it before there is anymore mischief."

Lin said, "We will."

"What's the best way to alert the American President's security detail?" asked Longinus.

Ross said, "If I go over there to the Hofburg Conference Center and do it, they will detain me.  So, the best way is to text message my boss General Matthews and let him relay the message."

Lin asked, "Are you sure he will?"

Ross said, "Yeah, he will.  He'll make sure it gets through."

"And what about Die Glocke?" asked Longinus.

Ross said, "Lin and I have to get over there and program the machine to take us back to Zurich to Emanuel's place.  Once we get there, I'll destroy it with the extra PETN explosives I stored in the garage."

Lin had used the Nazi time machine to escape the gun battle which had erupted last week at the Asiatisches Essen Philippine Restaurant in Zurich.  That was where she and Ross had been staying at the behest of their old friend, Emanuel Mesiyas.  Emanuel was the enigmatic Philippine taxicab driver who had shared many of their past adventures.

Longinus said, "All right, then that's the plan."

Lin looked at Ross and said, "It's the only way."

"But what about this Doctor Wu Qiang?  I wish we could take care of that little loose end," said Longinus.

Ross nodded.

"As much as I'd like to, I think we'd better count our blessings and just continue with our tasks," said Ross.

Longinus said, "I understand."

"Lon, what weapons are you carrying?" asked Ross.

Longinus reached into his overcoat and pulled out the QSW-06 Chinese pistol and the Italian Rizzuto stiletto.

Lin went to the room safe and opened it. She pulled out the Beretta and two spare magazines and handed them to Ross.

Ross said, "Thanks Lin. And you've got our ticket home?"

Lin opened her coat and showed Ross the SS dagger cinched behind her belt.

"All the way," said Lin.

Ross smiled. "I'll send that message now to General Matthews."

He scrolled up the phone number of his friend and started typing the following message:

Sir,

I believe there will be an attempt to disrupt the Presidential summit in Vienna this evening. President Trump and President Xi Jinping's lives could be in jeopardy. Please alert the US Secret Service immediately. The attempt could be from a rogue Chinese element. No time to explain everything now.

James Ross

Captain, SF

US Army

Ross pushed the send button and the text was delivered.

"That takes care of that," said Ross. "Let's go."

The three friends left the room and rode the elevator down to the lobby in silence.

Special Assistant to the US Ambassador Clive Maxsted was sitting in the lobby reading the Heute newspaper. He had been waiting for Ross to appear. The four members of his DSS team were strategically placed in the four corners of the lobby. They were waiting for Maxsted to give them the signal to arrest Ross.

When the elevator doors opened, Longinus turned to Ross and said, "I'll get my car and bring it around to the front."

Ross said, "Okay," and took Lin by the hand.

Maxsted saw Ross exit the elevator, and he put down his newspaper. He got out of the chair and walked over to confront Ross in the middle of the lobby.

"Captain Ross," said Maxsted. "Do you remember me?"

Ross searched his memory.

*Of course,* he thought. *This is the State Department guy I met in the Philippines last year. This is the idiot who tried to arrest me.*

Ross shook his head and said, "I'm afraid you must have me mixed up with someone else."

Maxsted said, "I'm Clive Maxsted, Special Assistant to the US Ambassador here in Austria." Maxsted produced his wallet credentials and showed them to Ross.

Ross said, "I'm afraid you're mistaken, sir. Right now I'm in sort of a hurry. If you'll excuse me." Ross took Lin by the hand and started to walk around Maxsted.

"Stop right there," said Maxsted. "Don't play games with me. You are Captain James Ross. And you have no authority to be operating in Austria. I have a DSS team waiting to arrest you for violating the Austrian Sovereign Neutrality Act."

Longinus had gotten his Audi from the parking valet and was waiting in front with the engine running.  He looked at his 1940 Eterna chronograph wristwatch.

*They should be here already,* he thought.  *Something's wrong.*

Longinus left the engine running and went back inside the Herrenhof Steigenberger Hotel.  He overheard Ross arguing with a man in the middle of the lobby.

Maxsted said, "You have no charter to be operating here."

Ross held Lin's hand and brushed past Maxsted.

"I told you sir, you are mistaken," said Ross.

The DSS team members were getting restless waiting for Maxsted's signal to move in and arrest Ross.

Special Agent Erwin Foxwell thought to himself, *Why doesn't Maxsted just give us the signal?  Why is he talking to the guy so much?*

Longinus walked up quickly and put his hand on Maxsted's left shoulder.

"You have made a mistake, sir," said Longinus quietly.  "This is my brother, Charles Inus."

Maxsted gave Longinus a startled look.

"What?" said Maxsted.

Longinus pointed to Maxsted's throat and to his abdomen.  He said, "If you don't get out of here and leave us alone, I'm going to split you from here to there."

Maxsted stopped talking and stared at Longinus.

Longinus looked at Ross and Lin. "Let's go," he said.

The three friends dressed in black hurriedly walked out of the hotel, leaving Maxsted standing alone in the center of the lobby.

Special Agent Foxwell got up from his chair in the corner and walked over to Maxsted.

Foxwell said, "What happened sir?  Is anything wrong?"

Maxsted, catching his breath, said, "Make sure you've got the target identified before you call me next time.  That man is not even James Ross!"

# CHAPTER NINETEEN

# A DEBT PAID

The late afternoon was cold with crystal puffs of wet snowflakes softly floating down and clinging to everything they landed on. The sun was setting, and its last rays were like a shimmering translucent blanket on the glistening white, waiting to be unfurled.

Longinus motioned to his Audi A5 Cabriolet in front of the hotel with engine running. He scrambled around to the drivers side (right side steering wheel of course) and let the heat of the interior cascade over him. Ross held the door open for Lin and she seated herself in the back, while he took the passenger seat next to Longinus.

Longinus said, "To the Burggarten, I presume?"

"Yeah," said Ross. "Next step is to get Die Glocke the hell outta there."

Inus engaged the clutch and shifted into first. He eased into traffic and sped up. Soon he was performing a flawless racing change to fifth gear as he passed a yellow Citroën.

*On to the Burggarten,* thought Longinus.

The Burggarten is a park next to the Hofburg. It originally was a Napoleonic battlefield in the early 1800s. The park is full of statues and monuments. There's even a Mozart statue which has a whole labyrinth of tunnels beneath it. The Hofburg was built in the 13th century and is located in the center of Vienna. It is the former imperial palace of the Habsburg Dynasty. Today, the Hofburg Palace is the official workplace and residence of Austrian President Alexander Van der Bellen. Part of its 59 acreage houses the museum, with 21 rooms filled with rare antiquities dating back thousands of years. Some of these include imperial treasures of the Holy Roman Empire, ecclesiastical artifacts of emperors, and jewel encrusted crowns of former kings and queens. The Spear of Destiny is also located there on public display.

*I've been guarding that spear for over two thousand years,* thought Longinus.

He downshifted and turned onto Ringstrasse.

*It's been my curse to guard it since I made that fatal error on Golgotha.*

*But now,* he thought, *I've got another chance to do something right. I can assist in stopping potentially what could be the matchstick igniting World War Three.*

Ross's cellphone began vibrating in his pocket. He pulled it out and looked at his text messages. The latest was from his friend General Braxton Matthews. It said he received Ross's message and was alerting President Trump's Secret Service detail about the threat at the Vienna summit with Xi Jinping.

"I just got a message from General Matthews," said Ross. "He says he's alerting Trump's security detail about the threat."

"Great news," said Lin. "That's absolutely great news."

Longinus gave Ross the thumbs-up.

Ross was smiling and glanced into his sideview mirror. He noticed the same red BMW sedan still behind them.

"Lon," said Ross, "have you noticed that red BMW behind us?"

Longinus looked into his mirror.

"Do you think it's the opposition?" he asked.

Lin looked up into the rearview mirror and saw the BMW.

*My God it never ends, does it?* she thought. *Just as we get a little break.*

Ross said, "Why don't we circle around the Hofburg a couple of times and see what this joker does?"

"Right," said Longinus.

Longinus was driving around Ringstrasse, when he suddenly pointed with his finger.

"There's the parliament building. Inside is where the Trump/Xi summit will take place," he said.

Ross said, "It's practically right across the street from the Hofburg."

Longinus said, "Yes. It only takes about two minutes to walk to it."

Ross glanced back at his mirror.

"The red BMW is still following us," he said.

Longinus nodded.

"My guess is it's the Chinese, because they used BMWs before in their attempt on the spear," said Longinus.

"That's right," said Lin. "The Mossad guys were in a black Mercedes-Benz."

"Okay," said Ross running over scenarios in his mind. "Let's get to the Burggarten. We need to get Die Glocke out of here."

Longinus shifted gears and the turbocharged 2.0 liter 4-cylinder engine roared. He quickly changed direction. The red BMW stayed closely on his tail.

In a few minutes, Longinus said, "There's the park."

Ross said, "Do you have the coordinates of where we originally picked up Lin in the park?"

Longinus said, "Yes I should."

He scrolled through his dashboard GPS. Then Longinus said, "Here we are."

Ross tapped the screen. "That's where we need to go. To those coordinates."

Longinus followed the directions into the parking area next to a snow-covered clump of trees, and just to the left of the barely visible Mozart statue.

"I see it," said Lin.

There next to the trees, scarcely visible because of the snow, rested the Nazi time machine codenamed Die Glocke. It was almost entirely covered with snow, thanks to a snowdrift which had been blown from the tops of the trees next to it.

Longinus placed the Audi in park but left the engine running and heater on.

*Bzzz.*

*Bzzz.*

*Bzzz.*

It was Ross's cellphone.

Just then the red BMW pulled into the same parking lot and stopped about twenty meters behind them.

Ross pressed the *answer call* button and placed the phone on speaker.

"Paradox," said Doctor Wu Qiang on the other end.

Ross waited.

"Paradox," said Wu once again.

Ross said, "You're finished Doctor. You've failed."

There was stunned silence on the other end of the call for a few seconds, followed by a smattering of Mandarin being spoken.

Doctor Wu Qiang said, "On the contrary Captain Ross, it is you who are finished, it is you who have failed. I don't know how you so quickly overcame my treatments, but you and your friends will die tonight."

Ross hung up the call.

"Come on," said Ross as he got out of the car.

Longinus turned off the Audi, then he and Lin followed suit.

"Outside gives us more maneuver room," said Ross, with his frozen breath rising in misty puffs and circling skyward.

They crouched down behind the Audi and both men drew their handguns.

The doors of the BMW opened and out came three men and one woman. All moved to the rear of the BMW, and one opened the trunk. Doctor Wu Qiang, Zao Konton, and Mei Fang now held Norinco AK-47 rifles. Boi Kyuki was holding an RPG rocket launcher

Then a black Mercedes-Benz sedan with tires sloshing and spitting snow sludge everywhere plowed into the parking lot.

The Mercedes skidded to a halt in front of the BMW, with high beam lights blinding the Chinese.

Wu yelled, "Who are these people?"

Zao held his hand up shielding his eyes from the high beams and said, "Probably CIA!"

Mei Fang decided she'd had enough insanity and dropped her AK-47 rifle to the snowy ground. She was thinking about making a wild dash to the rear, but decided instead to just throw up her hands in surrender.

Four armed men got out of the black Mercedes-Benz sedan and took up defensive positions. They were Yitzhak Zanir, Benjamin Shiloah, Shabtai Yatom, and Zvi Harel — the Mossad team. They were armed with suppressed Israeli Masada 9mm pistols.

Zanir yelled at the Chinese, "Drop your weapons!"

Wu barked to his comrades, "Guns in the trunk and get in the car now!"

Mei picked up her rifle out of the snow, and she followed Wu, Zao and Boi as they dropped their weapons into the trunk and slammed it shut.

Zanir yelled, "Drop your weapons and hands up!"

The Chinese were already in the BMW with Zao behind the wheel.

"Get us out of here!" yelled Wu from the front passenger seat.

Zao rapidly engaged the clutch and stick shift. The BMW started sliding on the ice beneath its tires and spinning its wheels.

Shabtai Yatom said, "Do we let them go sir?"

Zanir observed the sliding red BMW spinning its wheels and making for the parking lot exit.

"Yes," said Zanir. "Let them go. No need for blood this evening."

Ross, Lin, and Longinus watched the entire scene unfold in stunned silence.

"Wait here," Zanir told his men. Then Zanir turned around and started walking towards the Audi.

Ross peered through the falling snowflakes and saw the man approaching. He said, "Whoever just saved our lives is walking towards us. I think I'll walk out and greet him."

Before Lin or Longinus could say a word, Ross started walking towards Zanir.

Both men walked forward and soon stopped, each facing the other, in the no-man's land of the snow-laden Burggarten parking lot.

Ross immediately recognized Zanir.

"Yitzhak, my old friend," said Ross as he extended his hand.

Zanir smiled and shook hands with Ross.

"James Ross! Can't you ever stop getting into trouble?" laughed Zanir.

Ross said, "How ... where ..."

Zanir said, "I owed you one for Tempelhof."

Ross remembered back to when he was on the trail of international terrorist financier Wolfram von Lugoff, and the fight that had occurred with ISIS in Lugoff's hangar at Tempelhof airport in Berlin.

Ross said, "Oh, that."

Zanir smiled and said, "Yes my friend, we're even. Now take that damn machine and get out of here."

Ross quizzically looked at Zanir.

Zanir said, "Take Die Glocke and go.  Please."

"Okay," said Ross.  "But why?"

Zanir said, "I'm giving you this chance because you're Emanuel's friend.  Get out of here so I can make up an excuse how the machine slipped through our fingers.  But not before I say hello to Lin and whoever that guy is over there."

Ross smiled and said, "Come on."

Night began to fall on the ancient Napoleonic battlefield known as Burggarten.  Ross walked with Zanir back to the Audi and his friends.

"Lin," said Ross, "You remember Yitzhak, don't you?"

Lin was startled at first that somehow everything was good now, but quickly came around and said, "Of course.  Nice to see you again."

Zanir embraced Lin and said, "Make an honest man out of James, won't you?"

Lin laughed and said, "I will."

Then Ross introduced Longinus.

"And Yitzhak Zanir, may I present Lon Inus.  He's also a friend of Emanuel's."

Zanir held out his hand.  Longinus took it, and in the dark could be seen and heard a static electrical spark igniting between the hands.

"Wow," said Zanir chuckling, "looks like we've made a connection."

Longinus smiled.

Zanir said, "And how long have you known Emanuel?"

Longinus thought for a second.  Then he said, "I've known Emanuel Mesiyas before he was even born."

Zanir immediately broke out into laughter.

Lin and Ross looked at each other nervously and then started to laugh.

Longinus wondered what was so funny.

# CHAPTER TWENTY

# *TIMELESS PARADOX*

Zanir soon departed with the rest of the Mossad team.  They drove off and left Ross, Lin, and Longinus in the parking lot.

Ross turned to Longinus and said, "Lon, I want to thank you for everything — for saving my life — for everything."

Longinus looked at Ross with his sad dark brown eyes.  "Glad I could help.  I wish I would've been more watchful of the Chinese."

They shook hands one last time.

Lin embraced Longinus and then kissed him on the cheek.  "I'll never forget you, Lon," she said.

Longinus the Roman Centurian — pierced Christ's side at Golgotha with a spear — cursed to protect the Spear of Destiny until the return of Christ — friend to Emanuel Mesiyas and now James Ross and Lin Sparrow.  He was a man out of time.  Destined to wait, protect, and wait again.  But every now and then, he got a chance to right a wrong.  This was one of those times.

Longinus said, "My friends, take care of each other, and love each other. And if you can, keep in touch."

"We will," said Ross and Lin in unison.

"And next time you're here," said Longinus, "the French onion soup is on me."

Ross nodded. "We'd better get going," he said.

Longinus looked upward into the night sky. The snowflakes were floating down like so many miniature paratroopers.

"Good luck," said Longinus. "And safe travels."

Longinus turned towards his car, then turned back around.

"Wait a second. I've got something for you."

Then Longinus went to the Audi and opened the trunk. He came back with a broom.

"Here you go," said Longinus as he handed the broom to Ross, "for the snow on the Bell."

Ross took the broom and laughed. "Thanks Lon."

Longinus decided to wait to leave until Die Glocke had taken off. So, he sat in the Audi A5 Cabriolet with the 4-cylinder turbocharged engine humming.

Ross and Lin turned and started to trudge through the snowy field.

"There it is over there," said Lin pointing to a mound of snow by a small clump of trees.

Ross took the broom and brushed off the snow from the entrance hatch. The hatch had a circular submarine-type nautical wheel handle that Ross spun to the left to open. He pulled open the hatch on the machine that Heinrich Himmler had nicknamed *Die Glocke* over eighty years ago.

Ross turned to Lin and asked, "Ready?"

Lin responded, "Ready."

Ross stepped inside first and sat in the Luftwaffe pilot's seat. There was only one seat in Die Glocke, so Ross scooted into it as deeply as he could. It was a large step over the metal rim of the hatchway for Lin. She put her right leg through, ducked her head under the archway, and glided her left leg over. Lin sat on Ross's lap as he adjusted the straps of the *fallschirmjäger,* or "paratrooper" harness to accommodate two people.

"You'll have to close the hatch," said Ross.

Lin leaned forward and pulled the hatch closed. She spun the inside circular handle clockwise until it stopped. Then she tugged at it one more time to make sure.

Ross scanned the control panel searching for the *macht auf* switch, otherwise translated to "power on" button.

He flipped up the plastic safety cover and pressed the button, which immediately started to glow an ancient, amber luminescence. Then Ross set the trip parameters and the GPS coordinates to take them to the garage of the Asiatisches Essen Philippine Restaurant in Zurich. The grid coordinates function was a very primitive 1940s-era direction-distance-location dashboard map screen which allowed you to input latitude and longitude coordinates. There used to be a *gangschaltung* (gear shift) control lever with a Trolit Thermoplast button on top, which the time traveler would ratchet backwards or forwards depending on if the trip was to the past or the future. That lever had broken off in Ross's hands inside the Horten flying wing, so Ross made a field expedient replacement out of the SS dagger.

Ross looked at his Benrus watch. It was 1830 hours.

"The Trump/Xi summit is already in progress," said Ross.

Lin snuggled against him. "And you just saved the world my love," she said.

"We did," said Ross, "and Longinus. Go ahead and put the dagger in its place."

Lin took the SS dagger from her waistband and inserted it into the engagement slot opening.

Lin said, "We're ready."

"Let's go," said Ross.

Holding the dagger securely so it would not disengage or fall out of its slot, Lin ratcheted it forward.

*Clack, clack, clack.*

The sounds coincided with the spinning of the control panel grid coordinates dial.

*Clack, clack, clack.*

If Ross and Lin could have seen the outside of Die Glocke, they would have been amazed. The base of the machine was emitting a greenish-orange glow, and the entire outer capsule was starting to vibrate. The snow covering Die Glocke was quickly melting and giving off a hefty steam. The clacking sound inside was in competition with a swirling, rushing, windstorm sound outside growing in intensity.

Longinus was still sitting in his Audi, engine running, waiting for Die Glocke to disappear. But then something immediately caught his eye from the left. He noticed the flash, the streaking trail of smoke, and then the explosion.

*KA-BOOM!*

"What the hell?" said Longinus, sitting up and peering through his foggy windshield.

Die Glocke was in the process of vanishing and making its inner dimensional trip, when it was hit by an RPG rocket.

Then Longinus saw the red BMW, half hidden by bushes, far off to the left.

"Son of a bitch!" cried Longinus. "Goddamnit!"

Longinus put the Audi in gear and charged towards the BMW. He could see two people scrambling to get back inside. The rear of the Audi was whiplashing back and forth on the icy pavement, but then the quattro all-wheel drive tires gained traction and the turbocharged engine screamed as Longinus barreled towards the enemy. Like a man possessed, Longinus sent the Audi hurtling like a missile towards the BMW.

*CA-RUNCH!*

The entire right side of the BMW caved in, trapping the inhabitants inside.

Longinus calmly exited his Audi and pulled out his pistol.

Walking up to the BMW windows, he could see four Chinese startled faces contorted in pain.

*KA-POW!*

*KA-POW!*

*KA-POW!*

Longinus calmly shot three of them in the head. Blood and brains splattered across the interior. Then he quickly noticed Doctor Wu Qiang, the Warlock, sitting in the front passenger seat.

The Warlock was frantically pulling on the door handle.

*KA-POW!*

*KA-POW!*

*KA-POW!*

*KA-POW!*

*KA-POW!*

Longinus emptied his pistol into the Warlock's head. The BMW door that the Warlock had been so desperately trying to open slowly opened by itself, and the Warlock's lifeless body drooped halfway in and halfway out, restrained by a seatbelt. The blood dripping from his head stained the snow a dark red, and created tiny red snowflakes increasing in size.

Then Longinus turned around and started running towards where Die Glocke had been. He ran through the snow, fell once, quickly got up and stopped at the spot where Die Glocke had stood.

Standing there huffing and puffing, his lungs feeling like he was breathing razor blades, Longinus stared at the sizzling, steaming, crystallized sheet of glass that now occupied the earth where Die Glocke had once rested.

Longinus sighed deeply.

Inside Die Glocke, Lin and Ross were immediately flushed with an overpowering sense of peaceful bliss.

Fighting the almost irresistible desire to close her eyes, Lin focused her concentration and held the SS dagger securely in place. But the blast from the RPG had disrupted Die Glocke's electronic circuitry and telemetry, and they were rapidly spinning into the past.

Then both Lin and Ross lost consciousness.

The bottom gauge of the mechanical sprocket calendar was spinning wildly out of control.

… 27-NOV-2011 …

… 15-OCT-1999 …

… 21-SEP-1984 …

… 30-AUG-1972 …

… 13-JUL-1964 …

… 17-MAY-1957 …

… 20-APR-1945 …

Die Glocke — the Bell — had been equipped with a fail-safe device.  In the event of a lightning strike or other electromagnetic spectrum phenomena, the machine would return to a date designated by its creator.  In this case, the creator was Obergruppenführer Hans Friedrich Kammler.  The machine had returned to the Third Reich's Ministry of Science and Technology building, in Berlin.  1945 Berlin.

Lin and Ross slowly regained consciousness.

The blissful feeling Lin had experienced was suddenly replaced with a dull, throbbing headache.  It was like she had seasickness.

*Oh God,* thought Lin as she grabbed her queasy stomach.

Lin pulled the SS dagger out of its gear slot and slid it behind her belt.  Without that make-shift control lever, no one could use Die Glocke for time travel purposes.

"James," said Lin. "Are you all right?"

Ross groaned. "Ahhh.  Yeah, yeah I'm fine."

Lin said, "What do you think happened?"

Ross shook his head. "I'm not sure."

Then Ross looked at the mechanical sprocket calendar date wheel.

*20 APR 1945*

Ross pointed to the date. "That can't be right," he said. "Lin, set it to today's date and let's get outta here."

Lin reset the trip parameters and verified the grid coordinates.

Lin said, "The coordinates haven't changed. They were still set for Zurich Switzerland."

Ross said, "Okay then. Let's just make sure we're home before we open the hatch. Go ahead."

Lin inserted the SS dagger into its slot and pushed it forward.

Nothing happened.

"Oh boy," said Ross.

Ross unbuckled the seat straps and let them fall to the side. Then Lin reached forward and spun the hatch handle counterclockwise. She pushed on the hatch, and as it opened it let out a hydraulic hiss.

Lin stepped outside first, quickly followed by Ross.

"What is this place?" asked Lin looking around.

Ross scanned the scene. It appeared they were inside a huge warehouse, or perhaps an aircraft hangar. And they were alone.

"It looks like a large warehouse of some type," said Ross.

The place was huge. Probably ten thousand square feet. It had banks of high overhead fluorescent lights, and large steel-barred windows. There were long tables with various types of electronic equipment. There were industrial lathes, generators, and drill presses. Large wooden crates lined the walls, some were open and had spilled their contents to the concrete floor.

"This might be a laboratory," said Ross.

Lin walked around. She said, "Yeah, it might be some type of lab. There's electronic equipment, what looks like generators, and tables filled with test tubes and centrifuges."

"But this stuff is old," said Ross, "very old."

"Shhh," said Lin. "Listen."

Ross kept quiet and heard what he thought were the sounds of explosions and gunfire outside.

"Sounds like a battle," he said.

Ross walked over to a long table and noticed a newspaper. He picked it up. The newspaper was a copy of *Das Reich,* Germany's famous Nazi newspaper from World War Two. The paper was dated 19 April 1945.

Ross handed the paper to Lin.

"Take a look," said Ross.

Lin held the newsprint in her hands.

"My God," she said. "We're in World War Two."

Ross said, "Yeah. Berlin in April 1945, precisely."

"But how?" asked Lin.

Ross said, "Something short circuited with Die Glocke when we were traveling." Ross's eyes wandered around the warehouse. "And she brought us home," said Ross. "To her home."

Then his eyes froze on an object.

"Lin," said Ross pointing with his finger, "look over there."

Lin turned her head and saw it too.

There, sitting on wooden pallets, was another Die Glocke.

"Oh my God," said Lin.

Ross took her by the hand and said, "Come on."

Ross and Lin walked over to the other Die Glocke resting on pallets.

"This one is smaller," said Ross. "Not quite as tall as the one we came in on."

This prototype was indeed different than the one Ross and Lin had just arrived in. About the size of a small automobile standing upright, it was approximately six feet wide, and seven feet tall. It was made out of the same type of metal as the other Die Glocke. It looked heavy, probably three to four thousand pounds. Its color was a dark metallic gray. Electronic cables crisscrossed around its base and up to its top. There was the same type of hatch with circular nautical handle on the front. Circling around the top of the machine appeared to be small windows or reflecting mirrors. It was very reminiscent of Wernher von Braun's early design for the NASA Mercury space capsule.

Ross unhooked the cargo straps that were securing the machine to the pallets and threw them to the side. Then he spun the handle counterclockwise and opened the hatch. They both peered inside.

"This one still has its shifter lever," said Lin.

Ross said, "Yeah. Are you thinking what I'm thinking?"

Lin said, "You mean like we should use this one to get home?"

"Yeah," said Ross.

Then he closed the hatch.

"But before we do," said Ross, "let's take a look outside first."

Ross and Lin walked to a door on the near side. There were stenciled letters on the frosted glass window of the door that could only be read from the outside.

Ross opened the door carefully and looked at the words.

"Well, my German's a little rusty, but I think this says *Science and Technology Ministry.* And that swastika there pretty much proves its Nazi Germany World War Two."

They were indeed inside the large expanse of laboratory in the Ministry of Science and Technology building in 1945 Berlin.

Ross scanned up and down the hallway. There was no one in sight.

"The calendar in our machine said 20 April 1945, right?" asked Ross.

Lin replied, "Yes, that's right."

"If I remember my history correctly, that's the start of the Soviet siege of Berlin," said Ross. "Let's go take a look outside."

Ross and Lin walked down the hallway and saw an overhead sign proclaiming *Ausgang* or exit.

"This way," said Ross, pointing with his thumb.

Sounds of battle were echoing through the colossal marble foyer, and the overhead chandeliers were shaking. They walked down the foyer and came upon the entrance doors. Ross pulled the seventeen-foot-tall mahogany double doors open. What greeted them outside was unbelievable.

The scene was utter chaos. Berlin was indeed under siege from the First Belorussian Front commanded by Russian Marshall Zhukov. Smoke from artillery rounds filled the sky and streets. Buildings were burning. Small arms fire could be heard sporadically. Ross and Lin hurried down the concrete steps and took refuge behind what appeared to be a downed Panzer tank in front of the Ministry's steps.

"This is incredible," said Ross.

Ross saw an STG 44 Sturmgewehr assault rifle lying next to the body of a Wehrmacht soldier.  He picked it up and turned the body over searching for other weapons.  Ross pulled a Walther P-38 pistol out of the man's belt holster.

"Here," said Ross as he handed the Walther to Lin.  "Let's move to the other side."

Ross and Lin walked around the Panzer tank, keeping low, and saw a young boy in the fetal position clutching his rifle.  The boy was wearing an SS uniform indicating he was an Unterscharführer, or sergeant.  The boy was surrounded by the bodies of his dead comrades.

*Christ,* thought Ross. *He's just a kid.*

Ross knelt down and touched the boy on the shoulder.

"Hey," said Ross.

The boy immediately jumped up and started flailing at Ross with his fists.

"Take it easy son, take it easy," said Ross as he held the boy's arms.

Tears were streaming down the boy's face, but then he suddenly recognized the language Ross had spoken.

"You are English?" asked the boy between sobs.

Ross shook his head. "No. American."

Lin reached over and wiped the tears off the boy's face.

Ross asked, "What's your name?"

The boy said, "I am Ansgar Nachtnebel."  He was trembling with fear.  "I'm in the 3rd SS Panzer Division Totenkopf."

Ross noticed the boy was wearing an Iron Cross on his uniform.

*That's the medal for bravery in combat,* thought Ross.

"How old are you?" asked Lin.

Ansgar said, "Eleven."

Lin asked, "And how long have you been a soldier?"

"Four months," said Ansgar.

Ross looked at the bodies that the boy was surrounded by. They'd been shot to pieces. Some were missing legs and arms. Some were missing heads. Then he noticed the bodies in the street. Civilians. Many women. Old and young. Kids. They'd been sexually assaulted and butchered by the Red Army.

"How long ago did the Russians come through here?" asked Ross.

The boy was still shaking. "A couple hours ago."

*KA-POW!*

*KA-POW!*

*KA-POW!*

Ross pushed Lin and Ansgar to the ground behind the Panzer tank. He scanned the street and saw several Russian soldiers walking towards them, shooting at various corpses.

Ross whispered, "Four Russian soldiers, coming this way."

Lin pulled back the slide on her Walther P-38, making sure a round was chambered.

"They're mopping-up," said Ross. "Just stay down. I've got this."

Ross leveled his Sturmgewehr across the rear fender of the Panzer. He sighted in on the four Russian soldiers. Then he flicked the selector switch to semi-auto for more controllability.

*KA-POW!*

First, Ross shot the furthermost Russian soldier — in the chest.

*KA-POW!*

Then Ross shot the closest Russian of the team — in the face.

Now the Russians reacted and wondered who was shooting at them and from where.

*KA-POW!*

Ross shot the next Russian in the team.

The last Russian soldier made a break for it and started to run away.

*KA-POW!*

*KA-POW!*

Ross shot him twice in the back.

Ansgar had been watching Ross.

Standing up, Ross said, "Okay it's over."

Lin helped Ansgar up.

"Are you all right?" asked Lin.

Ansgar had tears in his eyes. He hugged Ross and said, "You saved my life! I'll never forget what you did! Those Russians surely would have killed us! You saved our lives!"

Ross wrapped his arm around Ansgar's shoulders and said, "It's okay, it's okay. It's all over now."

Ansgar looked up into Ross's face.

Ross asked, "Do you have a home to go to?"

Ansgar shook his head. "No. Dead. They're all dead. My father is a soldier somewhere. I haven't seen him in seven months. My mother ..."

Ansgar started to tremble again.

"... the Russians took my mother with them. I never saw her again. And my little sister was ..."

Tears came streaming down Ansgar's cheeks.

"My little sister was …"

Lin embraced Ansgar.

"It's all right, it's all right," said Lin.

Ross knew he and Lin had to get back — back to the future — back to their future.

Ross placed both his hands on Ansgar's shoulders and said, "You have to go home now.  Get out of here.  Your obligation to the military is over.  The war is lost.  You must go home."

Ansgar said, "But I have no home, not anymore."

The noise from the heavy Russian artillery was getting closer and closer.

Ross unbuckled his Benrus Type 1 watch and placed it on Ansgar's wrist.

"Here," said Ross.  "I want you to have this."

Ansgar looked at the watch and held it to his ear.

"Now," said Ross, "you have to go.  Keep going until you are safe."  Then Ross began to remember his World War Two history. "Head west," said Ross.  "Find the Americans or British.  Turn yourself over to them.  They will take care of you."  Then Ross shook hands with Ansgar.

Lin gave Ansgar a hug and kissed him on the cheek.

Ross turned to Lin and said, "Come on."  He took her by the hand and headed back to the Ministry of Science and Technology building.

Ansgar watched them leave.  Then he picked up his Mauser rifle and ran.

*I will never forget those two Americans,* he thought.

Ross and Lin sprinted up the steps of the Ministry building. They hurried down the grand expanse of marble foyer, and entered General Kammler's laboratory.

"Do you think it will work?" asked Lin.

Ross said, "It's got to, or we'll be living in the Twilight Zone for the rest of our lives."

Ross placed the Sturmgewehr rifle on the ground, and stripped off his suit jacket and sweater and threw them to the floor. He opened the hatch of the time machine prototype and adjusted the straps of the *fallschirmjäger* harness to accommodate two people.

"This one is gonna be a very tight squeeze," said Ross.

Lin took off her overcoat and wool jacket and dropped them as well. She hefted the Walther P-38 pistol in her hand.

"Maybe we'd better keep this one?" she said.

Ross looked. "Yeah," he said. "It wouldn't hurt."

Then Ross stepped inside the machine and squeezed his body as tightly as he could into the Luftwaffe pilot's seat. Lin stepped up and over the hatch rim and sat on Ross's lap. She leaned forward and pulled the hatch closed, turning the inside circular handle clockwise until it stopped. Then she tugged at it one more time to make sure.

Ross said, "The insides and control panel are almost exactly the same as the other machine."

Ross scanned the control panel searching for the *macht auf* switch. He flipped up the plastic safety cover and pressed the button, which immediately started to glow an amber luminescence. Then he set the trip parameters and the GPS coordinates to take them to present day December Zurich. The grid coordinates function was a very primitive

1940s-era direction-distance-location dashboard map screen, which allowed you to input latitude and longitude coordinates.

"We're all set," said Ross. "Go ahead and do the honors."

Lin wrapped her hand around the *gangschaltung* control lever.

"I love you James," said Lin.

Ross said, "I love you too."

Lin blessed herself with the sign of the cross, and then pressed the Trolit Thermoplast button on top of the lever. Then she ratcheted the lever forward and the time machine vanished.

# EPILOGUE

*The secret of happiness is freedom, and the secret of freedom is courage.*

Thucydides
460 — 400 BC
Athenian General

# TIME STARTS NOW

Zermatt is beautiful at midnight.  The lights from the town provide a warm, soft, comforting glow in direct contrast to the icy cold omnipotence of the Alps.  Zermatt is a town in the canton of Valais in Switzerland.  With a population around six thousand, Zermatt is world-renown as a mountaineering and ski resort that sits at the foot of the Matterhorn.  Nestled just outside Zermatt, on twenty prime acres of real estate, is the compound of billionaire Ansgar Ludwig Nachtnebel.

Ansgar was feeling every one of his ninety-one years today.  He had been informed through his intelligence contacts that his plan to eliminate the presidents of China and the United States had failed.  Along with that, all members of both Chinese teams had been killed, and that his good friend Doctor Wu Qiang was among the dead.  Ansgar stared out the panoramic window of his mountain chalet at the lights below in Zermatt.

*Everything was set,* he thought.

*The plan was perfect.*

*We had the patsy.*

*But somehow this American soldier turned everything around.*

"Would you care for a nightcap, sir?" asked Aemilius Urs, his trusted manservant.

Ansgar turned around and said, "Yes, yes I would. Bring me a Napoleon brandy."

Aemilius bowed. "Very good sir."

Then he scurried off to fetch the brandy.

Ansgar walked into his library. The room held his vast collection of treasures, from Egyptian art to Mesopotamian artifacts. The walls were adorned with paintings from Picasso, Degas, and Matisse. His library housed first editions of Hemingway, Steinbeck, Fleming, Cervantes, Dostoevsky, and Hugo, all of which lined the walls. But none of that meant anything to Ansgar, for this room also held his most treasured possession of all. The ownership of which made everything else of as little consequence. He walked over and stared at it in its glass display case.

Aemilius returned with the brandy and noticed his boss looking in the case.

"Would you care for me to remove it for you, sir?" asked Aemilius.

Ansgar said, "Yes. Bring it to me over by the fireplace."

Aemilius bowed and proceeded with his white-gloved hands to lift the glass covering and remove the object.

Ansgar seated himself in a plush leather-bound chair next to the grand fireplace. The crackling fire brought back memories of his childhood growing up in Berlin.

Aemilius bowed and said, "Here you are sir." He placed the object into Ansgar's aged hands.

Ansgar looked at the watch. It was a Benrus. Not at all unusual, as Benrus watches have been around since 1921. But this watch was special. It had been given to Ansgar by the only human being who had ever done an unselfish act for him. It was given to him in April 1945 by an American soldier. The soldier saved Ansgar's life from a Russian patrol in the streets of Berlin. A patrol that would have most certainly raped him before they killed him. This watch was very special indeed, as was the soldier who had given it to him those many years ago.

*But this Benrus watch holds a secret,* thought Ansgar.

He turned the watch over and looked at the inscribed date of manufacture.

*NOV 2020.*

Ansgar thought to himself, *How did an American soldier, during the siege of Berlin in 1945, give me a watch off his wrist with a manufacture date of over seventy-five years in the future?*

**THE END**

# ABOUT THE AUTHOR

Bernard Cenney retired from the United States Army as a Lieutenant Colonel after more than twenty-eight years in uniform. He considers it a privilege to have served his country throughout numerous command and staff assignments the world over. He makes Texas his home.

www.ingramcontent.com/pod-product-compliance
Lightning Source LLC
Chambersburg PA
CBHW030423310726
48979CB00009B/1587/J